Mitchell Forbes

Doctor Moledinky's Castle

A Hometown Tale

Also by Gerald Hausman

Prayer to the Great Mystery: The Uncollected Photography and Writings of Edward S. Curtis

Duppy Talk: West Indian Tales of Mystery and Magic

Wilderness (with Roger Zelazny)

Tunkashila: From the Birth of Turtle Island to the Blood of Wounded Knee

The Gift of the Gila Monster: Navajo Ceremonial Tales

Turtle Island Alphabet: A Lexicon of Native American Symbols and Culture

Turtle Dream

Ghost Walk

Meditations with Animals

Meditations with the Navajo

Doctor Moledinky's Castle

A Hometown Tale

Gerald Hausman

Simon & Schuster Books for Young Readers

SIMON & SCHUSTER BOOKS FOR YOUNG READERS
An imprint of Simon & Schuster Children's Publishing Division
1230 Avenue of the Americas, New York, New York, 10020

Book design by Paul Zakris
The text for this book is set in 12-point Weiss.
Manufactured in the United States of America
First Edition
10 9 8 7 6 5 4 3 2 1
Library of Congress Cataloging-in-Publication Data
Hausman, Gerald.
Doctor Moledinky's castle : a hometown tale / Gerald Hausman.
p. cm.
Summary: Twelve-year-old Andy and his best friend Pauly spend one remarkable summer in the 1950s exploring their town Berkeley Bend and delving into the secrets of its unusual inhabitants.
ISBN 0-689-80019-3
[1. City and town life—Fiction] I. Title.
PZ7.H2883Do 1995
[Fic]—dc20 95-5843

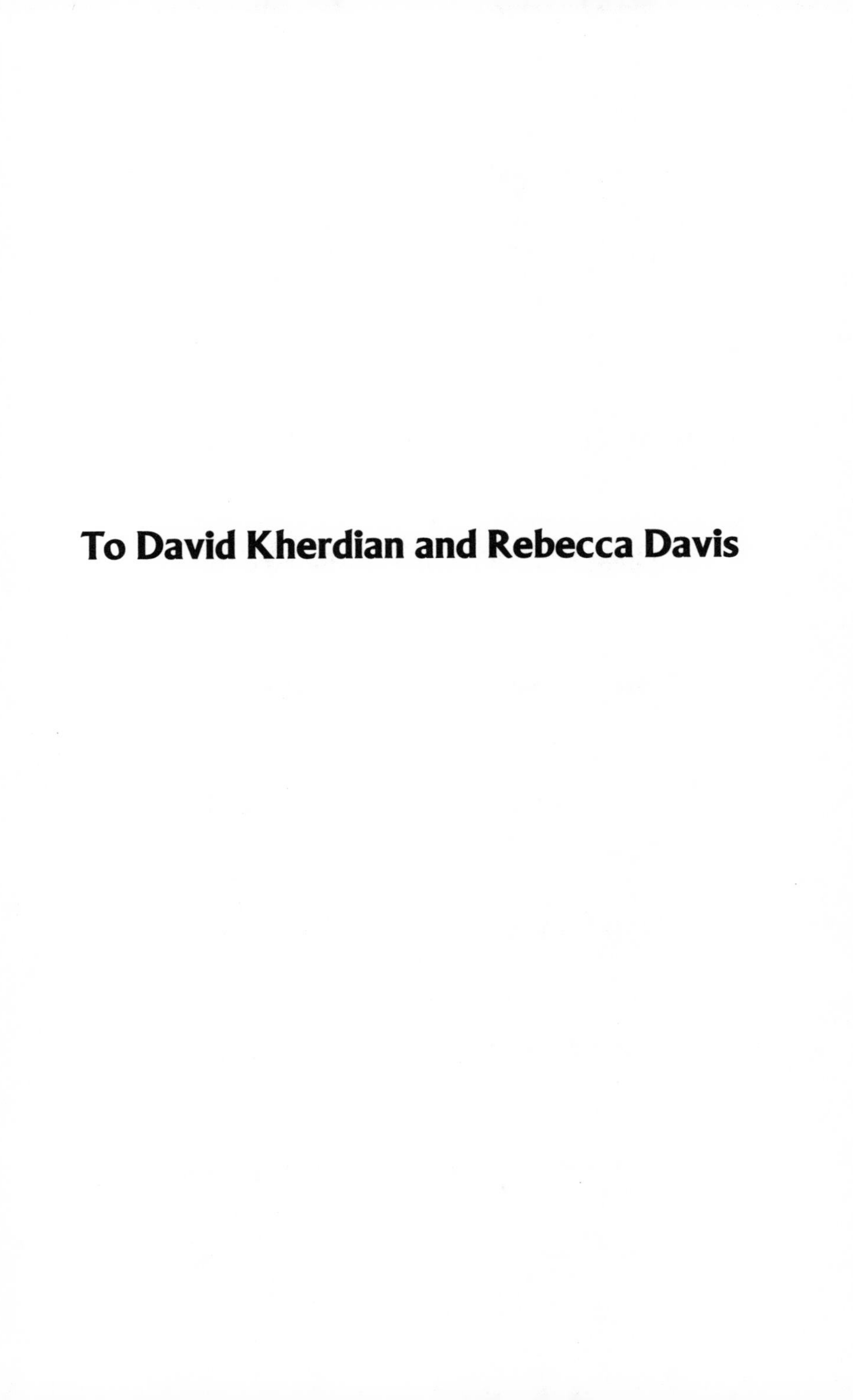

To David Kherdian and Rebecca Davis

Contents

My Neighbor Pauly, My Dad, and the Elephant

I live in Berkeley Bend, which is a town just like any other except, the way I see it, Berkeley Bend's a whole lot different.

One thing, it's a place of uncommon beauty—everybody says so. There's a mood here, too, a mixture of birch tassels and moss, hummingbirds' nests and cast-off snakeskins. There've been full-moon nights when, looking out the attic bedroom window of our house, I've seen fireflies spin and dance like whorls of moving moonlight. And once, during a heavy rain, I watched a blue heron land on a fence post, looking like our minister, Mr. McKinnon, about to deliver his Sunday sermon.

Possibly, though, it's the people of Berkeley Bend that are so special. They're not like others that you meet—why, Vito Mondelli was singing and dancing in the street while hugging a watermelon to his chest, a couple days ago.

And he wasn't drunk—that's just the way he is, and the way a lot of people are around here.

There's Mrs. Henshaw, who lives around the block from us

in an unfinished two-story tar-paper shack, sunk in wild briars that seem to hold the house in a green grip of iron.

And Old Ben, the bus driver who's everyone's friend, and who plays the Jew's harp to his chickens.

Dr. Moledinky is our one real millionaire—self-made, my dad says, and he lives in a real castle with a moat that has . . . well, we don't know exactly what's living in that thing, but you can bet it isn't guppies, because one time my best friend Pauly lost his dog and we found a pile of clean little bones right beside Dr. Moledinky's moat.

They were dog bones, all right.

So that's what it's like living in Berkeley Bend: The people here, as I've said, they're different.

But it still doesn't explain the way things are around here. You know, kind of mysterious. Even the land looks different from other places; the hills all folded neatly into woods with great spooky, spidery grayish oak trees glooming over the houses and casting a twilight shadow over everything.

And the houses: Some are small and peak-roofed like country cottages in storybooks. Others, especially in Italian Town, which is on the other side of the tracks from where we live, are bright green, pink, and aquamarine, and these look, driving by them on a Sunday afternoon, like a flowering of houses.

Now that you know something about Berkeley Bend, I want to tell you about my best friend (and next-door neighbor) Pauly Barlow, who claims the real reason Berkeley Bend's like no other place in the world's because of my dad's elephant.

Pauly says this gives a twist of magic to the neighborhood, the town, the people, and even the air itself.

Well, it would, it could—if only it were true.

But it isn't.

You see, my dad's elephant is imaginary.

The day after we moved to Berkeley Bend, last summer, Pauly came over to visit us.

Pauly walks up, knocks on our back door. No big deal, except I was sick in bed that day, and my dad got to the door before my mom, which is always a mistake.

My dad peeks out the window, and seeing a rusty-haired kid with a face peppered with freckles, he smiles.

He opens the door, and Pauly says, "The new kid at home?"

(He called me "new kid" for about a week, until he decided it was okay to call me by name, Andy.)

So my dad says, "He's down with a bug."

"Down where?"

"Down in bed."

"What's he doing down in bed—with a bug?"

You have to understand that my dad loves words with double meanings.

By then I'm up, getting a cold glass of orange juice from the fridge, and I see Pauly for the first time.

I am thinking: This poor kid doesn't know what a jokester and trickster my dad is. So I step up and introduce myself.

Whereupon Pauly says, not kidding at all, "Can I see the bug you were down with?"

Well, once you get to know him, Pauly's no stranger than anyone else in Berkeley Bend. Certainly no weirder than my dad and that elephant business of his . . . but that's getting ahead of myself.

Now, the following day I'm feeling a lot better when Pauly comes over for another visit. I see him coming through the hole in the hedge that separates our property, and I run for the back door, but unfortunately my dad gets there first.

My dad says, "Hello there."

"Hello," Pauly answers.

"So, what can I do for you today?"

"Is the new kid up yet?"

"Andy?"

"Who else is there?"

My dad replies, "Well, there's his older brother, Sam."

"So, is Andy up?"

"He was when I last looked."

Now you'd think my dad had better things to do than play word games with an eleven-year-old kid, but this isn't ever the case. So there's Pauly at the door and my dad standing so Pauly can't see me just behind him, and he's saying: "Andy's not available right now."

"Why not?" Pauly wants to know.

"He's tied up with our elephant."

"Who tied him?"

My dad grins. "Well, I'm just saying, Pauly, that Andy's indisposed—that is, busy." My dad, seeing Pauly's confusion, continues: "You see, he's feeding our pet elephant, tending to its toenails, and that sort of thing."

"Does Andy do that—all by himself?" Pauly queries. "I mean, does he ever get out to play, or does he just work all the time?"

My dad, appearing very serious, scratches his chin thoughtfully. "Sometimes he gets a little time off on Sunday," he remarks, chuckling.

"Well," Pauly sighs, "Tell him I was here, anyway."

Now is when I push my dad out of the way. And tell Pauly, "If you're going to be my friend—and I expect you already are—you're going to have to learn to ignore my dad."

Pauly frowns. "That wouldn't be polite."

And my dad pats Pauly on the back.

As you can see, they're quite a pair, aren't they? One talks serious; the other talks nonsense. But the way they do it, you can't tell which is which. They sound crazy some of the time, and just plain nuts most of the time. And you'd never guess in a million years that my dad was the creator of Build-em-Blocks, that construction toy like Lincoln Logs.

However, I get used to it—his kidding around.

The only thing is, I still can't convince Pauly to let go of that fictitious elephant. He maintains that we have it hidden away somewhere, some secret barn off in Watchung or Stirling, out in the country and away from town.

The other thing is that my dad's promised Pauly that if I mess up on the elephant's feeding schedule, he's going to appoint Pauly as the new caretaker.

Pauly really believes him, too.

That's what I like about Pauly, though.

He thinks the world's all his—and, when I'm with him, ours.

It seems when we're together that magical things do happen, which is why I'm writing this down; in fact, so much is going on this summer that it makes me wonder.

Pauly and I have promised ourselves that when we grow up, we're going to be the chroniclers of our hometown, the tellers of the tales that go on here that nobody knows about but us.

But I'm not going to wait until I'm grown-up to write about this weird summer of 1957. Why should I? I want to get it down now, while I can still remember it the way it truly happened, and the way it really felt.

You're probably wondering what I'm talking about. . . .

One morning I told Pauly that I thought Pam Snow was the prettiest girl in our town.

And he says, bright and quick: "You mean, in the looks department?" Then rolls his eyes, and lets out a sigh like a bicycle tire that was bitten by a nail.

I sing, "Pam Snow, Pam Snow, prettiest girl I ever did know," to the sweet tune of the cowboy song "Abilene."

But Pauly, discouraged, shakes his head. "I don't think you know her . . . not that anybody else does. . . ."

"Except you?" I throw back, indulging in a little shifty sarcasm.

Then I close my eyes, and I imagine the neat flowery dress she wore to school on the first day, the one with the frilly collar and the lacy sleeves, and I see her soft pixie face as if for the first time, and her shy, light-gray eyes, and her perfect nose and lips, and her crow's-wing hair, and her lovely white skin.

Oh, Pam Snow.

But Pauly's still frowning when I open my eyes.

I figure he can't accept Pam Snow ignoring him the way she does. After all, he's eleven and she's thirteen, about a year older than I am. And Pam Snow just doesn't speak to people under her age, unless they're little children, that is.

So that leaves Pauly, and all eleven-year-olds, out of the picture.

And it would leave me out too—were it not for some uncommon bond we developed when we first met. I don't know what it was or is—chemistry, I guess. One day it just happened in the lunch line. After that, we were friends.

You see, this is the way it happened: We are standing there, right after the noon bell that riddles your eardrums and rivets your bones, and we're getting our lunch trays, which are still hot to the touch from being washed, and smelling, somehow, faintly of meat-loaf gravy, and Pam Snow bumps her tray against mine, as a little joke that no one else can see, and she says, very whispery and sweet, "What're you going to have, Andy?"

Now, my name just slips off her tongue.

And she surprises me so bad, saying my name, that I am actually startled, and I jump a little in my skin.

Then we both laugh at the same time. Which makes us laugh again.

I'm looking for something to do with my hands, which are

moving about nervously, so I pick up a bag of potato chips from the lunch counter and, opening the bag with ease, pop a chip into my mouth.

Right away it catches in my throat; I start to choke.

Pam Snow's standing there, staring. Her eyes are widening, so that I can see the little bits of gold in the sleepy gray of her iris, and I'm thinking: What if I should choke to death, here and now, while staring into Pam Snow's beautiful eyes?

I'm thinking calmly, but I'm actually out of air. I'm gagging.

She's looking at me wonderingly—am I kidding or not?

Then I feel a thump on my back.

Thud!

Pauly to the rescue.

He's seen me choking, and he's run over and saved my life.

But even after it's over and I'm all right, I know I will never really recover from gagging like that in front of Pam Snow.

That is, until she reveals herself to be something other than what she is, or was.

So Pauly knew the truth all along, while I didn't, and probably it was because I didn't want to.

The real Pam Snow took me completely by surprise.

It was another unexpected potato chip out of the great bag of life.

Old Ben, Pam Snow, and the Blood of Summer

Old Ben drove the school bus every day. He picked us up and let us out, and walked us to the door of our house while his bus idled in the road. One time, when my mom was late getting home from O'Connor's Market, Old Ben stayed parked in front of the house. He smoked his amber-grained Missouri meerschaum pipe, and we waited—about thirty of us—until she drove up into our driveway. And, do you know, that whole busload of kids just sat and talked, and there wasn't one fight or any kind of disorderly conduct. That was Old Ben for you. He seemed to cast a spell of kindness wherever he went, and within its embrace everyone was safe from harm.

One day, however, all that changed—that was when Pam Snow came into our lives. But I'm getting ahead of myself again, aren't I?

Back to Old Ben: He had white hair, crinkly blue eyes, and skin brown as tanned pigskin. He was a heavyset man with a round, sad face, set off by big black bushy eyebrows. No one in Berkeley Bend was as good-natured as Old Ben; why, he was friendly as sunshine 365 days of the year. We always wondered why he had no kids of his own, because he seemed to love children more than anything. His yard was always full of wild-eyed kids and redheaded chickens.

I used to like to chase after Old Ben's feisty little bantams, the ones that lay those perfect, pill-shaped eggs, so small and white and impossible to find. They ran around between my legs, dashing fast like fighters on quick sprinty muscular legs, with their heads bobbing and weaving as they eyed you up and down and tried to get out of your way.

The ducks, though, were something else. They were never underfoot, but always nearby, floating like low-lying clouds and gabbing among themselves in duck-talk. Their eggs were everywhere, as if they had no particular use for them and they knew you were going to pick them up anyway.

On Fridays, all summer long, Old Ben killed chickens, plucked them clean, and sold them in town. That was the day Pauly and I waited for. We'd finish whatever chores we had around the house and run up in back of Bobby's house. Then run across the road and behind Hilltop Garage, to the big field that went straight to Old Ben's farmhouse.

If it was Friday, Old Ben would be out in his yard, sharpening his axe on a large stone wheel. He had taken an old bicycle that we nicknamed "the death bike" and put a sharpening stone on the front. He would sit on the bicycle seat, whirring the pedals, while his hands pressed the axe against the spiraling stone. The sparks looped away like fireflies into the shady summer noon.

"Howdy, boys," Old Ben would say from the leather seat of the creaking, groaning death bike.

"Howdy, Old Ben," we'd chime.

"Come to watch the killin'?" he'd ask innocently, his black brogan shoes circling beneath his bulk, whirling a low wind all around us. Those shoes were as much a part of Ben's image as his small-lipped smile. I guess you'd call them "Popeye boots," for that's what they looked like—great big balloon shoes that laced up tall. He kept them bright and shiny, and if a spot of dirt got on them, he quickly rubbed it off. When he walked, his brogans squeaked. Otherwise, for such a large man, he was quiet on his feet.

The bronze sparks nipped at our bare legs, tickling us. Pauly smiled with appreciation, and I smiled back. All week we'd waited for this moment. To us there was nothing morbid about it; the fact was, it was just plain fascinating.

"Well, I suppose this thing's sharp enough," Old Ben would finally say in his unaffected monotone voice. He got up out of the sharpener's seat and laid the axe in the bright green grass. Then he strolled toward the barn. We followed his snowy head into the tall, raftered darkness. Above our heads long blades of penetrating sunlight lay against the mounds of musty, dusty hay. Pigeons, hidden on the cross ties, cooed at our coming. The barn was much cooler than outside and the pigeon song was like cool water falling down on us from a great height.

Our job was to round up the stray chickens for Old Ben.

"The ones that are too hard to catch ain't ready to eat," Old

Ben sighed up ahead as he fumbled around behind his tractor. I flushed a blustery little bantam, who made good his escape out the door.

After a little while Old Ben caught a few; and then a few more. He dropped them into a burlap bag, and we held the bag shut while he went inside and fetched his Jew's harp. This was a ceremony with him, and for us a free symphony. We sat out in the yard, waiting for Old Ben to return.

Pretty soon he came out, a-twanging. "Dere-de-de-dere," the plucky harp went, and Ben rolled to and fro, like a circus bear trained for tricks. And the bear's grin was on his lips, as if savoring some old sweet, sticky memory of honey.

"What's that do?" Pauly asked the first time Ben ever invited us to a killin' in his yard.

"What, the harp?" Old Ben shook his wintry head, laughing deep in his chest. His belly bulged, shook up and down. And his small eyes, like green-bottle glass, twinkled in the sun. "Why, Pauly, don't you know the setup? First, the music—to soothe 'em. Then, the belly scratchin'—to set them up. Then, the killin', to let them off and finish the job."

That was how he did it.

A ceremony that made me think that the chickens knew it by heart; knew just what the deal was, and had, long ago, agreed to it.

After Old Ben twanged at the chickens in the bag to soothe them, he took them out by the feet. By then, they were all blinky, wondering what was going on, but not really afraid or anything. Then Old Ben laid them out, side by side, and scratched their tummies. One by one, each and every chicken fluffed out and went fast asleep. If you've never seen it done, maybe you can't imagine it: chickens all puffed out like pillows, snoozing in the midday sun.

Then Old Ben scooped them up, still sound asleep, and one by one he chopped off their heads.

Now, the moment the axe fell, the real magic happened—the thing that we'd waited for all week long. No, it wasn't the killin', so much as the second part. I don't know what name to give, except maybe the revivin', though nobody called it that.

Anyway, those dead, headless chickens sprang back up on their springy little feet and made a run for the woods. Naturally our job—Pauly's and mine—was to catch them. So we went chasing after these dead chickens. . . .

They didn't get far, but any distance gained by a dead chicken is pretty far where I'm concerned. As I was saying, the chickens would shoot off the chopping block, alert and alive and full of vigor, and head for the woods, running this way and that, with Pauly and me hurrying after them. One time one actually got away from us and we never saw it again. Old Ben said a fox probably got it, but every night for weeks we had scary dreams about that headless chicken roaming the back woods.

Well, that was Friday and Old Ben and the killin'.

We never thought anyone else knew about Old Ben's chicken killin', but one Friday morning when Pauly went out of town with his parents, I was riding my bike past Pam Snow's house, and she waved and asked me over.

"Where are you headed in such a hurry?" Pam Snow asked, her gray eyes widening with interest.

I flipped down my kickstand and caught my breath. One look at those dazzling eyes, and the potato-chip fiasco came back full force.

I pushed the disastrous chip out of my mind. "I'm heading up to Ben's," I told her. "It's Friday, chicken killin' day."

"Can I come?"

She asked so innocent and nice, I forgot to answer no, because chicken killin' is not for people like Pam Snow. But she caught me off balance and I heard myself say: "Why not?"

"Can I ride with you?" she cooed.

"Why not?" I said again (dumb).

She got on sideways. I raised the kickstand and began to pedal down the road, behind Sleazy Joe's Garage, across the field to Old Ben's. By the time we got there, Ben had already done the bagging.

"You're late," he commented, unsmiling.

"What's he doing?" Pam Snow whispered.

"He sings to the chickens first," I told her knowingly.

"Oh, no," Old Ben said. His face was stern, the summer glitter gone from his eyes. I'd never seen him look like that.

"Pam's all right," I said. "She's not afraid or anything."

Ben's usually smiling face had "no" written all over it.

Shaking his head, "What would your mother think," he muttered, "nice girl like you seeing a chicken killin'." It wasn't a question; more like a statement of fact.

"She doesn't care," Pam Snow said softly. Her voice was

pigeony, and calm. Perfectly calm, almost disinterested.

"Well—I care." Ben backed off, his voice trailing.

"I want to see," Pam Snow said earnestly.

"What girl wants to see blood splashing around," Old Ben remarked darkly. Again, not a question.

"I do," Pam Snow said. There was a sudden violet light, in her eyes, something that suggested a little more than mere interest. If I hadn't known her better, I would've imagined there was malice in those eyes. But I knew Pam better than that—at least I thought I did.

Old Ben's eyebrows rose, lowered. He turned, stepped closer to Pam Snow, looking at her inquisitively.

"You want to see blood and gore?" he asked, his black eyebrows raised high under his tan, wrinkled brow.

Pam Snow smiled, nodded pleasantly. Her calm eyes were trained on Old Ben's, and she didn't look away.

Then he turned and went to the death bike. He reached in the grass for his axe, ran his big brown thumb over the edge. Plucking a hair from his head, Old Ben put the blade to it—and, I swear, that white hair split in two.

Pam Snow gave a cooey little laugh, but her lips hardly moved at all.

Old Ben shrugged. Sighing, he said, "All right, so be it!" He went inside the house and got his harp.

"He's going to do it," I whispered confidently.

"I know." Pam Snow smiled. Once again I saw her eyes brighten and darken under the shade trees. Perhaps it was only my imagination, but in the quiet shadows of Ben's sleepy yard, I thought her eyes changed color. As I looked at them, they seemed to turn to a shade of plum, dark and hidden, and not friendly.

A moment later Old Ben started twanging on the Jew's harp. It didn't sound like it usually did; the notes were kind of somber.

He twanged.

I heard more cooing, but was afraid to look.

Then he took the drowsy chickens out of the bag and scratched their tummies, and they were all asleep. There was more cooing. And I felt a hand, cold as buttermilk fresh from the fridge, fit into my own.

I held my breath. I had her hand in mine. A tickly feeling traveled through me. I shivered briefly, and felt her hand grow heavier.

Old Ben placed the first chicken on the stump. Its eyes were wide open, staring dreamily into space. I saw one of its legs move very, very slowly.

The bright axe winked in the sunlight, rose, and lowered.

Pam Snow's hand closed tightly.

The dead chicken jumped from the chopping block to the ground and ran off into the summer air, flopping its wings.

My feet were numb, leaden; my hand was riveted by hers. I dared not move, hardly drew breath—waiting.

Then my hand was free, empty and open.

I saw someone dashing after the headless chicken. Standing stock-still, I looked at Ben. He shrugged. "Can't tell . . . with women . . . sometimes," he said under his breath.

Pam Snow ran through sun and shadow, chasing the chicken.

Old Ben shook his head, watching. The small bear's smile was back. Sweat trickled down his forehead. The air felt hot and thick, and for the first time it smelled of rank feathers and warm blood.

We watched her walking serenely through the cool shade, carrying the chicken by the wings. It seemed unnatural. Pauly and I always carried them by the legs.

I looked away.

Ben did too. Then he wiped the sweat off his brow.

"Well, that's it for the day. Looks likes rain, don't it?"

I nodded. It surely did. But before he got his axe wiped off and put away in the barn, and the dreaming chickens were back awake, Pam Snow had disappeared.

"Where'd that girl go to?" he asked me. "Looked away for a spell, and she was gone."

We looked at the chopping block where she'd placed the runaway. The wings were folded out in a grotesque manner. The neck of the chicken was dripping dark purple blood.

I felt my stomach roll.

Old Ben said only one thing after that. First he stooped down, picked up the dead chicken, and toted it by the feet into the house. Then he turned to me, and said: "I don't care who you bring next time, Bud, but see to it that they don't go stealing chicken heads." It was the first time he'd ever called me Bud.

Biking home, I felt sick to my stomach. In my mind, the purple blood was drip-drip-dripping on the grass, and the day was somehow spoiled. But I didn't—and couldn't quite—understand why.

At the same time, I kept remembering the way Pam Snow's hand felt in mine, as if it belonged there.

I was afraid I would never hold it again.

My mind went spinning around like the sharpening stone on Old Ben's death bike. Around and around.

What had happened? I wasn't sure that I knew.

There was Pam Snow's hand, soft as a snowflake, melting.

There was the blood of summer, spilling on the leaves.

There was that look of veiled violet in Pam Snow's eye; I saw it again now as my mind went on whirling. She had liked it, hadn't she? The blood, the killing time. And suddenly I knew what was wrong with me. For Pauly and me, those chickens running headless through the woods were almost dreamlike, something that happened but was hardly real; it couldn't be, for the dead don't walk.

In one swift moment I knew that Pam Snow's presence in Old Ben's killin' yard had made the whole thing real, very real. The purple blood would be spattered on those leaves forever. And so would her snowflake hand always be melting in mine as the summer leaves burned green as candles in the hot light of day.

Pauly, Prisoner of Tires

Pauly and I are always dreaming of the day we'll be able to drive a car. Sometimes we go into our garage, where my dad's old 1936 Buick is kept. It smells like ancient leather inside the car; the seats are all weathered and cracked, and there's a rumble seat in back, which also has a leather cushion to sit on.

The garage in summer is dry with dust because no one goes in there. The Buick is like a time machine—you can sit behind the wheel, and work the clutch and the gearshift, and imagine you're behind the wheel in 1936, when my dad bought the car new.

Pauly is shifting one day, and I notice he puts it into reverse, but he's pretending to go forward.

"What are you doing, Pauly? If you want to drive backward, you have to look backward."

"Naw," he says, "I can go anyway I want."

"Not if you want to drive a car like this someday."

"I'm not going to drive anyways," he remarks.

"But driving's fun."

"You can get into trouble," he laments.

"How?"

Shrugging, he says, "Not knowing how to shift, for instance."

"I can show you that right now."

"I don't want to learn."

"But why?"

There's no talking sense to Pauly when he's like this. He doesn't seem to care that in just a few years we'll be able to drive, and go anywhere we want, and do anything we want, and all because having wheels, as they say, is permission to be where you want to be, not just where parents say you have to be.

"You mean," I ask him, "you don't want to drive around and go to the car hop like my older brother Sam, and get chocolate malts on Route Twenty-two, and pick up girls at Bowcraft Archery?"

Pauly is entirely indifferent to the prospect. He's content, I suppose, to stay behind the wheel of our magic time-machine Buick rumble-seated roadster and just dream away the hours in the safety of our garage. Well, I don't mind it myself—since I can't drive on the road.

"I drove a car once," he says after some silence between us.

"Not on the road."

"On the road," he answers emphatically. "With my sister."

"You don't mean it."

"I do," he states flatly. "My older sister Judith let me drive her Sunbeam; you know, her sports car." He lets this sink in. That car, small and yummy, sits in my mind like a pretty strawberry. Which kind of fits with Judith as well. Awfully old, nearly twenty, I think. But a doll nonetheless.

"So you really drove Judith's Sunbeam . . . on the road?"

Pauly looks over at me, letting go of the wheel and scratching his head.

"Promise not to tell?"

"Who am I going to tell?"

"Your brother Sam."

"I won't."

Warily he sizes me up. Then: "Okay, I'll tell you. She drove me over to Hampton School. Then she parked in that great big parking lot and handed the keys over."

"Didn't she say anything to you?"

Pauly groaned a little. "She did. She asked if I knew how to shift."

"Did you tell her you could already drive a Buick roadster?"

"I told her."

"And she believed you?" I asked, amazed.

"Yup."

Suddenly I remember the dented back fender, the crumpled chrome bumper—the weeks that Judith drove her mother's Volkswagen while the Sunbeam was being fixed.

I said, "So it was you who wrecked your sister's car."

"She let me drive it, didn't she?" he snaps.

"Sorry, Pauly, I didn't mean to rub it in."

I feel a trickle of guilt. After all, Pauly and I—when we play, when we pretend—we imagine stuff that never happens. And we imagine it so well that, for us, it seems that anything we daydream about can turn real. Like driving the old Buick.

I'm the one that showed Pauly how to drive; I mean, make-believe drive. And he thought he could really do it.

The leather seat of the old Buick crackles as Pauly changes positions, folding his leg under him.

I pat him on the back.

"Don't worry, Pauly. It could've happened to me."

He stares blankly at the pine knots in the wooden walls of the old garage. Then, wrinkling his nose like a rabbit, he explains: "Andy, you showed me the H-shift pattern all right, but my feet don't touch the clutch, so I didn't know that part so well."

"You just push in the clutch when you're shifting. Otherwise you don't use it. You didn't shift without the clutch, did you?"

Pauly raises his shoulders and slides lower on the crackly leather seat. "Somehow," he goes on, "I got the Sunbeam into reverse, grinding the gears a good bit. Then I went backward—bumpety-bump, all the way up the front steps of the school, and crashed into the brick flower planter at the gate where you go in."

"Whoa! You did?"

"I did."

I can see red brick colliding into the red smoothness of the Sunbeam, and Pauly, so small behind the wheel of even that small of a car.

"Did you get hurt?"

"Nope."

"Judith?"

(I imagine Judith wearing a white hospital gown.)

"Nope."

And that was all Pauly ever said about his first experience behind the wheel. Sometime after that, we began to spend a lot of time up at Sleazy Joe's Garage, learning about customizing cars.

This was much safer for us, somehow, than imagining to drive them.

The fastest car in the neighborhood is Ray Romano's '52 Ford, which can wind out all the way to fifty-five miles an hour in second gear. Ray has a four-barrel carb and duels out the back, and big black heavy skirts over the whitewall tires, and best of all, the front of his hood is emblemless—smooth as a blacksnake's belly—with crimson flames painted front and back.

Herbie Belen's got a fast car, too—a Studebaker Golden Hawk, the kind with the upthrust fins in back that are definitely hawklike, winglike, and like nothing else in the world.

That's a humdinger of a fast car, and everybody says it's souped up plenty, and they always say it "hops like a bunny," even though it's a Golden Hawk they're talking about. . . .

But there's always a bunch of guys up at Sleazy Joe's, working on old cars, customizing them, taking the stock parts off and putting on the extras, and we like to watch them work and talk.

Mostly what they do is strip off the excess chrome while they channel the car down and sleek it up. They say it's "stock" before they strip it clean; afterward they say it's "honeyed out."

That's the way the guys talk about cars.

Like they were girls or something; and they give them girls' names, too: Big Deb and Li'l Lu and Saucy Sally.

Sleazy Joe doesn't mind us hanging around, so long as we don't bother him and stay out of trouble. But sometimes that's impossible, like the time Pauly got locked up in the garage after five.

He was poking around a pile of tires—Sleazy Joe has a great, tall stack of them, going all the way up to the ceiling—and Pauly slipped into them and couldn't get out.

But he wouldn't say anything either—not a peep was heard from him—so when quitting time rolled around and no one could find Pauly anywhere, we figured he'd gone home a long time ago.

I had my doubts, but he wasn't anywhere around.

Well, he was trapped in there, upside down, at closing time.

Prisoner in a ring of Firestone tires.

Sounds pretty scary to me, even now. . . .

"What'd you do?" I ask Pauly, later on.

"Well, I kicked and kicked," he says.

"Did that do anything?"

His brown deer's eyes blink, go blank.

"Nope," he tells me.

"So what'd you do then?"

"Upside down—I couldn't do anything."

"So you . . . just . . . stayed there, a prisoner of tires?"

He smiles. The freckles having a party on his cheeks.

"Being upside down wasn't so bad," Pauly explains.

"But I bet being in Sleazy Joe's Garage in the dark wasn't any fun—"

Pauly says, "Aw, it wasn't so bad."

"I bet it was—you're just not telling!"

However, he insists it's okay, because his parents hardly ever pay any attention to him, and whenever Pauly gets lost like this, his father goes crazy looking for him. You see, his folks are always fussing over his sisters, Judith and Betty. Most of the time they pretty much ignore Pauly. So when an opportunity comes along for some real attention, he goes for it. Getting lost, for Pauly, is as good as being found.

Anyway, Sleazy Joe's was a fun place to be, unless Joe was cleaning out his grease pit, in which case it was the greatest place to be in the whole world.

"Good thing your dad called Sleazy Joe and got him to open up the garage and they found you in that tire ring. Otherwise you might have been in there all night long." I was imagining Sleazy Joe's Garage after hours—all goopy and strange, and full of greasy stuff that lives in the pit at night.

Pauly admits, "Could've been scary, but it wasn't, really. My dad came and got me, and a couple days later he bought me a fully endorsed Red Ryder BB gun—just for the heck of it. He said he'd be a lot happier if I stuck around in the yard shooting tin cans, and I did—that day."

We are allowed to visit Sleazy Joe's even after Pauly's mishap because, at closing time, Joe always puts his head into the prison ring of Firestones, just to make sure Pauly's not in there trapped.

One day, though, Pauly fell into a worse mess than a bunch of rubber tires.

That was the day he fell into the pit.

Sleazy Joe Wormwood and the Pit of Death

Sleazy Joe's Garage was right around the corner from where Pauly and I lived. We walked through the oak woods by way of Bobby "The Streak" Sandler's old gray barn, and across the street was Sleazy Joe's.

The moment Sleazy Joe laid eyes on us, he said, in that nasally voice of his: "What do you kids want now—a little peek at Marilyn?"

Pauly said, "We dropped in to see the flames Ray put on the front of his Ford."

But also—just as Joe guessed—we were hoping for a little look at Marilyn. That is, Sleazy Joe's brand-new calendar of Marilyn Monroe in a solid-gold bathing suit. This was the only thing in the garage that Joe hadn't lacquered with grease.

We weren't the only ones who liked looking at Marilyn. Lois Bagley was our age, and she liked looking at her as much as we did. She said it gave her ideas. It gave us ideas too.

Well, there we were looking at Marilyn, and Sleazy Joe was working on a little Nash Rambler—the model that looked like a clown car at the circus. Ray Romano and his brother Randy and Jake Russell were down in the pit, cleaning it out with push brooms and solvent.

The pit was underneath the lift that raised up and held suspended the cars that Sleazy Joe worked on. It was an eight-by-ten-foot, squared-off cubicle that collected all the gunk and grease from automobile innards. Joe just spilled the guts out of those cars, and the pit ate them up—well, almost, anyway. There was a process to cleaning the pit that was worth the price of being kidded by Joe and accidentally getting an oil smear on your new Roy Rogers and Dale Evans T-shirt.

When we came into the cool churchlike atmosphere of the garage (I always thought of it as a kind of cathedral myself), Sleazy Joe was wiping his face with a woman's pink nighty. It was kind of filmy looking at the top, and the moment I saw it, I looked away so I wouldn't have to see Joe mopping his face with it. Pauly did the same.

Sleazy Joe was, hands down, the sorriest looking guy in Berkeley Bend. His front teeth stuck straight out and his lips were always apologizing for them by trying to cover them up. Joe was a Berkeley Bend original, a one-of-a-kind piece of work.

And that wasn't the only odd thing about his face. He had ears like a donkey and hair like a collie dog, and none of this would've been so bad if it weren't for the fact that Sleazy Joe Wormwood fancied himself a lady's man.

You see, some guys have it all—like Ray Romano: good looks and nice manners and an easy way with people. And some others, like Sleazy Joe, were lacking in just about every department. Yet he acted like women were fighting over him, like he was the best catch in town, the only bachelor in Berkeley Bend.

We'd watch him, Pauly and I, and he'd be like Sir Galahad of the Pumps whenever a woman drove up to get gas. It was probably more tragic than comic, but we couldn't help laughing. There was Joe, bowing grandly before a '56 Ford Fairlane, pump in hand. You would see the bright lipstick smile of the car's owner as Joe went through his romantic act, waving that gas nozzle like it was his dragon-slaying lance and grinning, ear to ear, making a perfect fool of himself.

He didn't know, of course, that everyone was laughing at him behind his back, making fun of him. Poor Joe. He believed, in his heart of hearts, that he was Victor Mature, whose face alone made women quiver with desire. Well, he was innocent—you had to give him that. And if he was a fool, he was at least an honest one.

But when he said, "Hey, fellas, you want to see a snapshot of my new girlfriend?" the guys down in the pit, mopping up the latest oil spill, guffawed.

Sleazy Joe wasn't laughing—he was serious.

Pauly came up, poised at the very edge of the pit, his white legs and coppery hair standing out against the dark, oily atmosphere of the garage.

Pauly, who always felt more than a little sorry for Joe, ignored the laughter, and said: "Hey, Joe, I want to see."

The funny thing was that Joe never seemed to notice, or to

mind, the fact that his employees made fun of him. They saw his antics with women, his courtly manner, as being ridiculous, and sometimes they laughed right in his face. Joe, for his part, never blinked an eye at this. I guess, to Joe, he was the greatest; people could laugh if they wanted to—Joe knew who he was.

But I'm not sure we did; not really, anyway. I thought of him as sad—and funny, at the same time. You never knew what he was going to say or do, but somehow it was always at his expense. I guess, like a lot of other guys, I thought he was silly. Why couldn't he see that he was just a ten-time loser whom no woman was ever going to swoon over?

Why couldn't he just see that?

It was plain as the oil on the end of his nose.

Well, anyway, Sleazy Joe came around the bumper of the Nash and reached into the rear pocket of his forest-green uniform pants. Fumbling, he produced his wallet and, cracking it open, peered into its papery depths, selecting a five-and-dime snapshot of a woman who was grinning like a marlin into the camera lens.

"You're lookin' at my new girl." Sleazy Joe whistled proudly. His eyes rolled around the garage, hunting for approval. But the place was as silent as a cemetery. Ray, Randy, and Jake pushed their brooms—*cha-fiff, cha-fiff*—across the floor of the pit. I saw them smirking, as usual, and I wished—just then—that Joe actually had a girl whose picture he could tuck into his wallet. Maybe I was the only one who wished this for him, but I did.

"Are they getting ready to hose out the pit?" Pauly asked. I think he was hoping to change the subject, because if Sleazy Joe went on about the girl, the guys in the pit were sure to tease hell out of him.

"You two want to watch?" Sleazy Joe asked, tucking the wallet into his back pocket.

"Sure we do," Pauly responded, glancing eagerly in my direction. I nodded confirmation. Truly, there was nothing more interesting than watching Sleazy Joe turn on the hose that pumped the chemical solvent into the pit.

Whatever gum and goo that was stuck to the pit's cavelike walls would get eaten up in a second. Joe's cleaning solvent was like a million little piranha fish that devoured anything that was sticky, tacky, or gooey. Pauly and I—whenever Joe wasn't looking—tossed little bits of junk in there to watch them dissolve. Pretty soon those goopy, oil-spilled walls were going to look shiny and new.

Joe said, "Hey, look out now, stand back. One drop of this stuff in your eye, and you'll be blind as old Lemon Jefferson." We didn't know who that was, but neither Pauly nor I wanted to be like him—no way. So we stepped back.

Ray, Randy, and Jake started up the ladder, their chunky engineer's boots with the metal cleats on the bottom making music on the iron rungs. They were all done in the pit; now it was time to scour it with solvent.

Pauly and I waited for Joe to throw the toggle switch that released the magic chemical from a spout in the wall of the pit. Out of that six-inch copper mouth the wicked fluid ran, bubbling and spurting, lemon yellow, smelling like hard cider and Babbo Cleanser and Renuzit Remover and half a dozen other unmentionable things.

"Don't get so darn close!" Joe hollered at us.

I backed up a step or two and waited for him to adjust the flow. Pauly, waiting for Joe to turn his back, crept up a little closer to the edge of the pit.

"Look," Pauly said brightly. He held up a writhing tent caterpillar. "Bet he needs a bath," he said.

Pauly took another step toward the edge of the pit, holding the caterpillar between his forefinger and thumb. It was wriggling to get away.

"You're not going to emulsify that thing, are you?" I asked, knowing full well that he was.

Sleazy Joe was checking the valve on the solvent pump when, all of a sudden, two amazing things happened at the same time.

First, Pauly, about to send the caterpillar to its doom, leaned too far forward, slipped, and fell directly into the pit. Second, just as he did that, the stream of yellow solvent began really flowing.

"Oh, no!" Joe shouted. "I can't shut the valve down."

"Pauly, get out of there—*now!*" I cried.

Jerking off my T-shirt, I extended it to him. Pauly jumped up to catch it, but it was slightly out of his reach. He was standing on a little island of metal filings, and the yellow solvent was seeping all around him.

He hopped up again and tried to catch the T-shirt.

"No time for that!" Joe yelled.

Then he jumped into the pit and, without thinking, jammed his skinny fist into the mouth of the solvent pipe. The urine-colored stream lessened to a trickle, dribbled, stopped.

At the same time, Pauly caught hold of my shirt and I pulled back hard; and with Ray and Randy grabbing on to my waist, we hauled Pauly out of there. Hard to believe, but he still had that caterpillar between his fingers. The edges of his Keds Racers were all eaten away, though, just like he'd been dunked, real quick, in a piranha bath.

"Did you get any in your eyes?" I asked.

Pauly shook his head. "I inhaled some fumes," he said, his face white as Mrs. Maury's picket fence.

Ray Romano screamed, *"Joe!"*

There he was, eyes shut tight, fighting the pain. He had shoved his whole hand and arm into that solvent pipe, and it was now socketed there as if for good.

Jake Russell snatched up a tire iron and started beating on the toggle switch. But Ray, always the smart one, ran around back of the garage and did something to shut off the power. There was a great sucking sound from within the pit pipe, and as the pressure was released, Sleazy Joe Wormwood began to fall slackly against the wall, his head lolling toward the floor.

The sickening chemical was eating at Joe's waffle-stomper boots, climbing upward, filling and swelling the deadly pit.

Then Ray and Randy dragged Joe up by the collar of his shirt, and Pauly and I looked on, amazed, as that little bantam guy gave us a quick smile, a fluttery wink, just before he passed out.

I looked up above him and saw why he smiled—like a guardian angel hovering over him was the calendar of Marilyn Monroe. She was all rosy gold, smiling, as it seemed, down at poor Joe. And you know, to tell the truth, they didn't look half bad together.

It was several days before the news of the loss of Joe's right arm, and his subsequent recovery in Plainview Hospital, was announced in the *Courier Dispatch*. The article was headlined GARAGE MECHANIC SAVES YOUTH, LOSES RIGHT ARM.

But that wasn't the end of the story, no sir.

You see, Joe had a slow recovery but a quick return, if you know what I mean. After what happened, he became the great hero of Berkeley Bend.

The Little League asked him to throw out the first ball with his left hand. The Rotarians asked him to speak about courage and its effects on citizenship. The Boy Scouts begged him to be a scoutmaster. And Dr. Moledinky brought his 1947 Buick Dina-Flo sedan to the garage to be serviced.

But none of those things meant much to Sleazy Joe. What meant the most to him was that the girl whose picture was in his wallet actually asked him to marry her. Yes, she turned out to be the real thing, a wonderful woman who saw Joe for what he was, a funny little man who loved grease but whose heart and soul were bigger than the Empire State Building.

I suppose Pauly and I always knew that Joe was greater than

he seemed, and that was why we forgave his girly-games and make-believe manners. But now, married, he became a different person.

For one thing, he backfilled the pit about halfway full of sand. And for another thing—no more piranha solvent. Once a month Ray and Randy and Jake shoveled the greasy sand into wheelbarrows and dumped it out back.

That was the time Pauly and I liked best, because you could flip a match at that huge pile of putrid grease, and tiny blue flames would come dancing up out of the black ooze like the sandsnakes of Mars that Flash Gordon was always fighting on Saturday's late matinee.

I don't think Pauly ever said another word about what had happened in the pit; nor did Sleazy Joe. But the two of them used to drink chocolate malts together, and Joe always had a sour-ball jawbreaker for Pauly, and one day I saw Pauly put something in his left hand. I never asked what it was, but it looked like a key ring with a plastic caterpillar on it.

I always wondered about that—not that it made any sense: Sleazy Joe's last name, Wormwood, and what happened in the pit that day. It was hard to believe, though, that Sleazy Joe used to be the man everybody liked to make fun of, when in truth he was the one Marilyn Monroe was smiling at all along.

My Dad, the Bridge, Vito, and the Crowbar

My dad's short as a fireplug, so people say. But he's also handsome, which kind of makes up for it, I guess.

But Pauly always says my dad looks like Sgt. Preston of the Yukon. You know, the TV show about the mild-mannered Mountie who, no matter what, always brings in his man.

My brother Sam, who's three years older than I am, says our dad looks more like the Cisco Kid than Sgt. Preston. But he says that most likely because he likes the Cisco Kid and Pancho better than anything else on television.

Well, my dad does look like some kind of cowboy, anyhow; at least we think he does, and that's all that counts.

My dad's always saying, "Don't take life so seriously." There are times, though, when I wish, as the saying is, he'd just grow up. Well, that's what he's always telling me to do, but then half the time he acts like a clown. This isn't surprising because his favorite pastime is going to the circus. He really lights up, too, when the clowns come on.

One time my dad takes Pauly and me to the Roy Rogers

Rodeo in Madison Square Garden. On the way we have to cross the George Washington Bridge.

My dad pulls up to the toll man. "Bridge safe?"

Giving my dad a glance over his eyeglasses, the toll man counters, "Course it's safe—what you expect?"

Pauly says, "I've been across it plenty of times, Mr. V."

"I'm not sure," my dad says vaguely. "What's it made of?"

Horns are beginning to sound behind us.

"Well," the toll man sighs, tipping back his hat to show the mark where it's bitten into his skin. "I suppose it's made out of little steel wires all woven together. Does that satisfy your curiosity?"

He stares, I think a bit mournfully, into my dad's eyes.

Pauly laughs. "I think the bridge is safe, Mr. V.—really it is."

My dad looks at Pauly, then at the toll man, and says, "Just tiny wires, you say?"

The toll man answers, "Think you could move along now, pops?"

My dad still seems a bit uncertain. "I think I'll let the decision rest with my uncle here," he says, nodding in Pauly's direction.

"Okay," Pauly pipes up. "I'm not sure the bridge is safe, but I'm willing to take a chance. Aren't you, Andy?"

I look at the massive structure before us: all those melded ropes of flexed steel gleaming ruby red in the setting sun. What a bridge, I think. What a colossal, magnificent, momentous, and amazing thing this bridge is!

My dad, on Pauly's cue, pays the fare, and without further

delay we drive on over the great fire copper bridge that spans the brown cloud-reflected river.

"Next time"—Pauly winks at me—"I'm going to personally guarantee the reliability of any bridge—before we get to it."

We listen in silence to the tires on the singing steel and all around us the ropes of wire burn in the dying sun.

Pauly whispers to me, "Hey, Andy, the bridge is holding up okay, isn't it?" Then he chuckles.

And my dad cracks a smile for the first time. "You know, Pauly," he remarks, "I think we're going to get across safely. But if we don't, I just want to know one thing."

"What is that, Mr. V.?"

"Can you swim?"

Pauly, unsmiling, says: "I personally guarantee it."

The next day, Pauly and I are outside in the yard, listening to the cicadas singing in the beech tree, when Vito Mondelli, the fruit vendor, pulls into our driveway with his creaky truck full of fruit.

Now, I like Vito all right, and so does Pauly, but whenever he shows up, no matter what, he yells really loud, "Having a fiesta?" to let my dad know he's there. When the two of them get together, it's worse than the elephant, or the George Washington Bridge. . . .

My dad says to Vito, every time: "You mean a siesta, don't you?"

Whereupon Vito repeats, "A fiesta!"

My dad's about the same height as Vito, and though Vito's

kind of heavyset and my dad's rather trim, they, being short, can look right into each other's eyes.

"So, Vito," my dad starts off, "what about the bank job? . . ."

He inspects a fresh blond apricot that Vito's plopped in his open hand.

Immediately my dad bites into it, and smiles with glowing satisfaction.

"Vito, that peach of yours is sweeter than money," my dad remarks.

"You mean that apricot of mine is sweeter than honey." Vito grins, showing off his great and marvelous gold tooth.

"Fiesta, siesta—who cares?"

My dad bites his apricot and wipes his mouth with the back of his hand.

"Vito," he says morosely, "I think we're going to have to put off robbing the bank for a little while."

"What for?" Vito asks.

"I've got to get myself a bigger crowbar."

"What about the tire iron that I keep in the truck? Ain't that big enough?"

"Won't do," my dad answers dryly.

Vito polishes a fresh apricot on his sleeve and pops it into his mouth, pit and all.

"You eat the pit, Vito?"

"Nope. Spit it out, after." Chewing some more. "How big's that bank vault, anyway?"

"Oh, I haven't been in it yet, but it's a large one all right," my dad replies. "And the door is cast iron. Bet we could crank away at it all day long and never get it open. We have to have the right tools, Vito, or the deal's off."

Vito squints and rubs the back of his hand against his stubbly bluish cheek. "You're the inventor, you oughta know."

"Thermodynamics, Vito," my dad explains.

"Nuclear physics." Vito nods.

And the two of them switch to peaches, and after that they step onto the back porch and speak softly about the surprising thickness of bank vaults and the weakness of crowbars and the fact that bridges aren't a bit safe anymore.

Pauly concedes to me, "You know, I thought they broke the mold with your dad, but that Vito's got him beat!"

"Ever been to Italian Town?" I ask him.

Pauly picks up a hard little crab apple that has fallen from our tree, and pitches it into the air.

I catch it, we throw it back and forth a few times, then Pauly replies that he seldom crosses the tracks, except with his mom, shopping.

"Never on your own?" I ask pointedly.

"Nope." He pockets the crab apple. "I would, though—with you."

I tell him that I've gone downtown and crossed the tracks with my older brother Sam, and I've visited Vito and his mother and even worked in their garden with them when the tomatoes needed harvesting.

"What's it like?" Pauly asks.

"Over there it's friendly all right, but you've got to know someone first—you know, like Vito."

Pauly nods, and I can see that he feels left out, not knowing Vito the way I do. "You think they'd like me over there?" he queries.

And I tell him, "Pauly, they like you everywhere!"

However, afterward, when I get to thinking, I decide that you have to prove yourself when you cross those tracks. It's not like other places in Berkeley Bend. If you want to make friends in Italian Town, you have to know the right way to do it.

I started out trying to talk like my dad—you know, kind of crazy, like he does with Vito. Only it didn't work out for me.

Not at all.

The Italian kids my age are suspicious, when I try to be offhand with them; I guess they figure I'm making fun of them, even when I'm not.

I'm just trying to make friends the only way I know how. But it doesn't really work out for me until the day I go up against Joey the Jolt. He's the toughest Italian guy there ever was or will be.

After that, though, the wrong side of the tracks are suddenly right. And I'm not afraid anymore.

Bobby the Streak and Joey the Jolt

One day Pauly and I were playing mumblety-peg, that game where you throw a penknife while doing splits. The way it's played is this: Two guys face each other, one with a penknife in hand. The object is to throw the knife so it sticks in the ground just outside your foot—a hard thing to do. Whatever the lead guy throws, the second player has to maintain and better. So you can end up with some pretty painful splits, which is the object of the game: getting the other guy so stretched out that he can't throw anymore without losing his balance and falling down.

Now Pauly was losing (his legs were shorter than mine), and he was saying: "You know, if I just had longer legs, I bet I could outrun Streak."

"Nobody," I said dryly, "can beat Streak, not even Joey Delmonico."

"Nobody's ever seen them run against each other."

"They don't have to," I said, throwing my knife far afield of my left leg. "Streak'd beat him."

Pauly fetched the knife, wiping the blade off on his blue wide-wale corduroy pants. The game over, I folded it and put it into my pocket. Looking through the woods that screened the yards between my house and Streak's, I noticed he was out there training, doing quick little wind sprints from his porch to the woodshed and back again.

"Hey, Pauly," I suggested, "how's about you and me go on up to Streak's house and see if he'll teach us a trick or two."

"It ain't tricks," Pauly exclaimed. "Streak's fast, that's all."

We watched Streak fade across his yard; he was a blur, a leg-whirling maniac.

"There's a trick to everything, my dad says. I bet we could learn a thing or ten from old Streak, specially if we bribed him. . . ."

"Bribe Streak—with what?" Pauly asked.

"How about your pump-action Red Ryder BB rifle?"

Pauly looked cross-eyed at me. "You mean let him have it—just like that?"

"Naw," I said, "kind of let him borrow it . . . in exchange for some tricks."

Pauly exhaled loudly. "Nothing doing," he remarked, wrinkling his nose. "Hey, I know—how 'bout your Whammo steel-ball, self-contained slingshot?"

My eyebrows went up defensively. "Loaner or a giver?"

"Neither." Pauly smiled. "We just take it up . . . as bait, kind of."

I nodded. "He'd probably go for it."

"Yeah, he'd go for it," Pauly confirmed.

Well, I had two of them—there was the old one my uncle had sent me, and then the newer one I'd earned on my own by selling greeting cards.

So I went and got my old Whammo slingshot, which looked new enough because I kept it so well, and Pauly and I walked through the oak woods to Streak's house. He was running so fast, when we popped out by his woodshed, he nearly knocked me down.

"What'd you do that for?" he said thickly. His long blond hair spilled like honey over his forehead and tweaked the base of his nose. Oh, what hair it was! Thick, slick. The style called a D.A., that is, a Duck's Ass, because it looked like one. Long in front, straight back on the sides, curved and parted behind the head. That was the D.A., and only true hoods wore them, cool guys with perfectly bad manners.

We waited, admiring his locks, while Streak got his breath.

Pauly, who was always the first to say something, said: "Boy, Streak, I wish I had hair like that."

Streak reached into the back pocket of his jeans and took out a small black comb, which he used to retrain the curl in front, sweep the sides, and duck up the back; then he shook out the whole thing with a sudden twist of the head.

Streak smiled coyly—he was really shy. Tough-shy, if you know what I mean. He was a real loner, the kind of guy you never see talking much. He liked doing streaky things, like running and wrestling and beating up guys bigger than he was. Most of all, though, he liked running, which was how he got the name.

"What're you guys up to?" Streak asked. He had a sleepy way of talking, whispery and soft, and a little sad sounding. But I always figured it was a cover-up for how fast he was with his hands and feet. But his hair—that was his best trick of all, the gleam of spun gold. Who cared if it wasn't real?

His eye fixed on the Whammo in my right hand.

"What's that you got there?" he whispered.

"Whammo," I whispered back.

"Hmmm," he mumbled. "Mind if I try it once?"

"If you show us how you run so fast," I said boldly.

Streak cracked a smile, which slipped away fast. He didn't like smiling, because it gave too much of his shyness away, and he liked to keep it, like most everything else, to himself.

"Kind of a trade, like," he mused. "Is that it?"

"Yeah," Pauly agreed, "like a trade."

"What I just said," Streak whispered, with a gentle hint of malice.

"So," I said, "you show us how you run, I'll let you borrow the Whammo." I knew, though, that the moment it left my hands, I'd never see it again. But that was all right. I had the other one.

Streak grimaced, his lip curled.

"What if I just step over and take that Whammo," he said slyly.

"That'd be all right too," Pauly said, shrugging.

Streak laughed. "Don't worry." He patted Pauly on the back. "I wouldn't do that to a couple of neighbor kids."

"You'll show us your trick, then?" I asked.

"What trick?" he answered, acting offended. But he was playing coy again, I figured. His handsome hooded eyes darkened only for a second; then they cleared, crinkled up at the corners, and he smiled.

"What if I was to tell you guys"—he paused, thinking—"my big secret. What would you gain by it?"

"Well," I said, "I guess every time I crossed the tracks down by Italian Town, I wouldn't be scared of Joey 'The Jolt' Delmonico."

Streak caught my eye, laughed. "You're afraid of that windbag?"

"You bet," Pauly put in.

Streak's green eyes glittered with amusement, then dropped back into soft, sleepy focus.

Slowly he reached into his back pocket and took out a small tube of ointment. Squeezing some in his palm, he let us take a good look at it. Then he told us to smell it, which we did.

"My secret," he revealed, chuckling softly.

Pauly glared, dumbfounded.

"Brylcream?" he said doubtfully. "Common old Brylcream hair oil?"

"No other, no better." Streak rubbed the little grub of white ointment into his forward-falling curls.

Then he offered the tube to me, and I took some. And rubbed it into my hair.

"Rub it in good," he advised.

I handed the tube to Pauly, who squeezed a white worm of

the stuff into his palm and began to wax it around his head.

Both of us rubbed it in well. It felt heavy, oily. Very heavy, very oily.

Streak took his special black pocket comb and handed it to me. Then, soft as the September breeze, he chanted: "Fried, dried, laid to the side."

"What's that mean?" Pauly asked, his hair all fountained up in front so that he looked like a rooster.

"Means you gotta look c-o-o-l," Streak said. "Slick-back-lean-mean-an'-cool . . . cool as a kite, cool as a shiv, just plain cool," he sang.

His hand flicked, snatched the comb out of my hand.

"Gimme that," he said. "Now you know Streak's secret. How 'bout that Whammo?"

There was something about that comb, though, some residual Streak-magic on it that rubbed off on me. I had felt my feet get lighter as I used it. They had seemed to rise off the ground with each electric stroke of that enchanted comb.

Now I felt a tingling sensation in my toes, as if they were twitching and itching to get to a race—any race. My arches arched, my hair dipped down, I leaned into the wind and felt the breeze blow through my bones and make them ring.

"Ahh," Streak whispered. "You feel it?"

"I do."

"The magic . . ." he mumbled, rubbing his palms.

"Yeah," Pauly echoed. His red hair was frozen into a coxcomb of flame.

We stood for a moment then, like two new-headed, fast-footed demons born to cross tracks, born to run like blue winds among the gray clouds.

"Do you really feel it, Pauly?" I asked.

He grinned, and nodded. His hair was a dollop of lava, boiling but not moving.

Streak snapped the Whammo, testing the action.

Then suddenly, businesslike, he nodded to each of us and walked back to his house, humming. He never looked back, not once. Nor did we; we made for the tracks. Walking, of course, so as not to overtax the magic.

Now, the other side of town, the wrong side of the rails, was a place that we both feared and admired. This was Italian Town, so named because it was founded and run by immigrant families, most of whom had come from Sicily. Many of them, the older ones especially, didn't speak English. They worked in the hot sun among the tomato-plant jungles, and they laughed and cursed and sang as did no other people in Berkeley Bend. They were alive, they knew it, and they celebrated it in everything they did.

So there was a freedom in Italian Town that you felt coming into it. It was a place where you could breathe the air all the way down to your toes. Yet there was only one problem: Pauly and I weren't Italian. It was well known over there, as Joey Delmonico used to remind us in the school yard, that there were only two kinds of people in the world: "Italians," he said, "and those who wanna-be."

Joey was more than a symbol of the freedom and isolation and foreign laws that governed Italian Town. He was the whole peppery place rolled up into pegged pants. Always, when we crossed the tracks, we saw Joey. He was always there, like a light post hanging over us. His favorite line out on the playground was "Okay, hotshot, give me your best punch." And he let people pop him in the belly, or even the face. Then he'd flatten them and leave them lying on the ground.

By luck, I guess, Joey had never bopped me the way he had other kids, but once I saw him smack Pauly for not showing Joey his marbles fast enough. Pauly had them in a little leather bag, and he fumbled as he tugged open the drawstring. So Joey open-palmed him across the forehead for being too slow. Pauly had a handprint on his pasty forehead for the rest of the day. That was Joey, all right; that was Joey, all wrong. But that was Joey.

Now we could feel the tippy-ends of our hairs beginning to dry out, but it was okay because by the time we touched down on Springfield Avenue, which was the official entrance of Italian Town, we were ready for anything. You stepped over the tracks, the silver rails, and all at once you were in another country; you were in the vineyards of Sicily.

First thing, just over the tracks, I bent down and tied my Keds. Pauly did the same. Then we strode by Delia's Liquors, past the crooked drainpipe by Antionetti's Motors, up the sidewalk past Giovanni's Barbers with the pole outside whirling in the sun.

And walked—right smack into Joey Delmonico.

For a moment he didn't do anything. He looked to the side,

as if something was coming from that direction. I looked too, but there was nothing there.

"Get lost, doughface," Joey said to Pauly. He gave him a smack, open hand, hard on the head. It sent Pauly sprawling. He was sitting on the sidewalk, his Streakified hair all mussed up, a look of bewilderment on his face. With one blow Joey had ruined Pauly's magic hairstyle.

Now, Joey still hadn't traded a glance with either of us. He was looking at something far off that we couldn't see. That was his special style—never looking at the thing he was really looking at.

Suddenly he put his left arm loosely around my neck, as if we'd been friends for around a hundred years. I staggered backward, tried to slip under his embrace, but Joey's arm fastened about me, tight as a snake.

He squeezed.

I choked.

Then, smiling, he cranked up his right fist and chunked me hard in the belly. I jackknifed, doubled on myself, dropped next to Pauly on the pavement.

Joey laughed. His blue-black hair flashed. His thin mouth writhed with amusement. But, always, his little blueberry eyes were dead serious.

"Look," he said toughly, as if his mouth were full, "who said a couple of cute guys like you was invited to wear your hair like that, huh? Who said?"

Pauly shrugged. Then he glanced absently at Joey, who folded back the cuff of his shirt and spat on the street.

I felt the anger rise up suddenly.

"Bobby 'The Streak' Sandler—that's who!" I said.

Joey's eyebrows rose in amusement. He knelt down beside me. I saw the crease on his pegged pants, his white socks, and low-slung loafers. These shoes were his special trademark. They were black, squeaky clean. The front part above the toes was creamy white. Dancing shoes they looked to be, but he always wore them, day in and day out. They had metal taps on the heels, which everyone called cleats. People said Joey never took his shoes off, even when he went to sleep at night.

Then I saw his balled-up fist—but before he could plant it a second time, I jumped up, almost knocking him down.

And ran. Like a bolt of blazing blue.

Pauly was right behind me.

I felt the wind tickling my hair, then the roar of blood in my ears as we raced down Springfield Avenue, past Vito Mondelli's vegetable truck with the open canvas sides full of shiny fruit. Vito waved at Pauly and me. "Hey, boys," he cried, "where's the fire?"

His answer came quicker than words—the cleated soles of wild, mad Joey Delmonico, head down, aiming for murder, lusting to pound us into the ground.

I opened up.

A streak before my eyes, myself reborn as Bobby. Flying high past Romano's Bakery.

"Can't . . . keep . . . up!" Pauly gasped, falling back, veering off by Prince's Deli.

Joey passed him, *clickety-clack,* smacking the back of his

head, open handed, as he shot by, not missing a stride.

I was wet—was it raining?

My hair felt cooler and smelled sweeter than one of Vito's peaches. Was I really flying?

And Joey kept coming on, coming on, coming on.

Then I went up on my toes and sprinted. The cinders flew, the locusts sang. We zoomed up Snyder, soaring across the swamp road that led to home. Joey the Jolt just behind me.

I burned. And when I snuck an over-the-shoulder look for the last time, it seemed that there were three Joeys wavering on the wind. So I pounded on up the road.

"You—gonna get it—ya little—!"

I didn't look back. He was there, murdering me with his mouth. But I steeled my nerves and wouldn't look back.

Then *herrash, shump, karroom!* I looked back: Some twenty Joeys, sun-blurred, slid on the gravel, went down in a pile.

I caught my breath, grabbed my knees, and snatched some air.

And saw a single broken-down Joey, calling for me to give him a hand. Help him up.

Joey the Jolt was lying in the road, cheeping like a little bird. "How 'bout a hand?"

Looking at him, the one of him, I could forget the two-fisted, bad-sided greaseball of the railyard afternoon. Now there was just this bent-up guy lying on his side, asking for help.

I walked back to where he was folded up in the gravel.

"Friends?" I gave him my right hand, hauled him to his feet. He came up weakly, his feet scratching for footing.

"Friend," he said, sucking wind, leaning over, bent double.

After a moment when all I heard was Joey's wheezing, he looked up, all sweaty-faced and red.

He tried to smile, couldn't; kept breathing loud, forcing air into his lungs.

"How'd you do that?" he puffed, his eyes burning into mine.

"What?"

"Run like that," he rattled.

"Hair cream."

He moaned, and it sounded like he wanted to laugh, but it was too much effort on top of his heavy breathing. So he just looked at me, his eyes shining. There were patches of road dirt on his hot red cheeks. A cataract of sweat was washing off his face.

"Don't tell nobody—" he said, clearing his throat. He looked at me, then: "Don't go around saying you beat . . . Joey the Jolt."

He paused as he said this, as if he himself were amazed at his words—and he was, I could tell that he really was.

"I won't tell. . . ."

"Hey, kid," he said gloomily. "Don't think I can reach 'em."

"What do you mean?"

"My loafers," he said hoarsely. "Can't bend down to clean 'em up."

I dropped my eyes to Joey's feet and saw the famous trade-mark loafers with the white calfskin, all scraped and scuffed and covered with road dust.

Joey's eyes were pinkish from fatigue, and little runlets of sweat wandered around his chin. He wiped them off; more came.

I don't know why, exactly, but I got down and brushed the road dirt off Joey's favorite shoes. I wetted my hand with some spit and buffed them a bit. The scuffs were deep—to the grain—but the dust and dimpled dirt came off quickly and restored the loafers to something of their original shine.

"Hey, kid," he said.

I said nothing.

"You're . . ."

Again, I waited for him to continue.

"Hey," he said, "you know, you're some kid."

"That's what my mother tells me," I told him.

Joey laughed, then coughed.

"Sorry I punched you, pal," he said. "It was a mean trick, but you know what my mother tells me?"

I shook my head.

"She says—"

I finished it: "You're some kid—right?"

He chuckled, rubbing his knuckles on his lower jaw. He looked about vaguely, staring into the blue sky as if he'd never set eyes on it before.

"You okay, Joey?" I asked.

It was then I knew I'd never used his first name to his face.

He tossed me a half-smile.

"So you won't tell, huh?"

Briefly his eyes met mine.

"No, Joey, it's our secret."

And it has been—right up until now.

Influences Good, Bad, and Elemental

My mom is critical of most people. Sometimes I think it's because her mom died when she was young and she was raised by her stepmother, who was a very proper English lady.

Anyway, my mom's always done things her way and is no less demanding, in her own manner, than my dad. She uses a stick she found in an apple orchard to prop up the oven door. My dad complains that the hinge just needs to be fixed and he'd like to do it for her, since he makes his living as an inventor. But she still prefers the prop-up apple stick.

She's always out in the woods gathering moss and planting it all around the house, and when I say: "You're going to cover us up in graveyard moss!" she answers, "At least we'll end up green." Which doesn't make much sense unless you know that green's her favorite color. Everything's got to be green in our house—emerald drinking glasses, chartreuse shades, grass-colored carpeting.

I suppose my mom would love little green men, too, if she knew any, but fortunately she doesn't. Normally, when she isn't out on a moss-gathering mission, she's complaining about the company I keep. Not Pauly, of course, whom she loves. But the others. One of these is Bobby the Streak, who's older and lives two houses up on Plainfield Avenue. She says he is nothing but a bad influence.

She goes on about him too, like this: "When you read in the *Reader's Digest* about boys with loose morals who go on wild escapades, those boys are exactly like Bobby the Streak."

I explain to her that Bobby's nice, really he is. But you have to get to know him first.

She says, "When you read in the *Reader's Digest* about people whom you have to know first, so that eventually you will like them, then you are dealing with the 'lower element of mankind.'"

I am always wondering what the "lower element" is, because to me it's as indefinite as the Holy Ghost or something.

So I go and ask my brother Sam, and he explains it this way: "She means low-class types—the kind that you and I like to hang around with."

"Is Pauly a low-class type?" I ask.

"He's too innocent to be of any class at all," my brother answers.

"But I really don't hang around with anybody else."

"You hang around with Joey the Jolt sometimes."

"Yeah."

"Well, that's what she means by 'lower element.'"

Sam doesn't care what my mom says, though. He always does what he wants to do, and if he gets asked questions later on, so be it. And the thing that drives me crazy is that she lets him get away with it!

Now, if it's me doing anything low and elemental, or whatever she calls it, then there's hell to pay. She never gives me any slack at all. Which is, I suppose, what you get for being born second in line.

My mom is something else. She went to the best boarding schools, and she learned to walk very straight with a book balanced on her head, and she speaks very correctly because she used to be an English teacher, and she believes in things like lower elements.

She wants us—our family—to be like the fine people she reads about in *Reader's Digest*. But my dad is always confounding her with his foolishness, and my brother Sam is always getting into trouble by talking back in school. However, nothing pleases her—and unnerves her at the same time—as much as my dad when he's playing a joke.

Like the time he goes off to work with his shoes on and a tie knotted around his neck, but the rest of him naked.

He's got the briefcase, the tie, the shoes.

But that's it, nothing else.

And he's heading out the door to go to work.

Pauly is having breakfast with us that morning and he looks up at my dad, who salutes him, Sgt. Preston style, very sharp and crisp, and my dad reminds Pauly that the elephant needs some extra rations of hay.

"Fine," Pauly says, smiling. "You tell me where you keep him and I'll toss him some hay."

Pauly doesn't seem to notice that my dad, but for the tie and shoes, is naked.

My mom's frying eggs at the stove, pretending nothing out of the ordinary's happening.

But there's my dad, heading off to work, naked.

She glances up from her frying pan, sees the emperor's new clothes, and lets out a little gasp, which is all part of the gag, I guess.

Anyway, then my dad leaves the kitchen and goes into the hall, and my mom follows after him, offering him her apron.

My brother starts laughing.

I laugh too.

But Pauly just keeps eating his toast.

I wonder what he's thinking—but how can you tell?

Then he says to me, still munching his toast, "Andy, is your dad really going to work like that?"

My brother howls.

But Pauly's very serious.

Sam claps a hand on his shoulder and explains, "Dad'll go as far as the front door, then he'll say, 'Hey, I forgot my wallet!' and he'll go back into the bedroom and get properly dressed for work. Hey, Pauly, it's all a big act, don't you see?"

Pauly cracks a small smile. "Like the bridge?"

"Like the bridge," Sam says.

Pauly says, "Is that how it is with your family?"

Sam nods, laughing.

We both laugh, but Pauly's still serious.

He says, "You mean your mom never gets mad at him?"

"Never," Sam insists.

Pauly shakes his head in disbelief.

"It's a comedy routine," Sam explains. "My mom's the straight man."

Pauly looks thoughtful.

He says, sadly, "I wish my mom and dad played around like that. Instead, they fight all the time. Real fights, not play ones. They go at it something fierce."

Sam and I say nothing. It's hard to imagine other people's parents doing things like fighting fiercely when they've always been nice to you.

We listen to my parents teasing each other in the hall. Then my dad says, "Oh, no, I forgot my wallet."

Pauly's got a big smile on his face now.

"Could I live here with all of you?"

Sam says, "You already do, Pauly."

And I'm thinking how lucky we are, having two such parents, who are always playing and never fighting, and it seems to me there's nobody quite like them.

But I find out otherwise.

There is one couple about as crazy—no, they're crazier by far. I'm talking about the Cooneys, who live right across the street. They are not really funny, but strange; and not as strange as they are weird.

Pauly and I walked their dog for them every day, until one dark summer night when all of Berkeley Bend discovered what Pauly and I had been guessing all along, that Mrs. Cooney's got magical powers. Maybe she's not a witch, exactly. But what do you call a woman who sees into the future, and talks to trees, and has secret meetings underneath her kitchen table?

Mrs. Cooney's Summer Lightning

The home of Mrs. Cooney, made of gray fieldstone, was low to the ground and hunched like a rabbit. The cedars that grew around the windows leaned close, sealing out the light and keeping in the darkness. Mrs. Cooney told me the trees spoke to her at night, whispering at the bedroom window. She was always telling us, Pauly and me, of her dreams, of things lost and gone, and soon to come.

Every morning we walked Mrs. Cooney's bulldog, Kendrick.

Since he was tied up most of the time, our little walks were his only freedom from collar and chain. The moment we showed up in front of his doghouse, Kendrick galloped in place. He'd pawed a deep gully in the ground at the place where his rope ended. Pauly and I would set him free, and he'd shoot away into the woods, with us running after him.

By the time we caught up to him, we were back on the Cooney property, having run at least a mile in a full circle.

Anyway, Kendrick was named after Mrs. Cooney's husband,

who was also named Kendrick. They both looked pretty much the same, only from what I can figure, Kendrick the man never got away from Mrs. Cooney. If he ever ran in a circle, it was on the living-room carpet.

Mr. Cooney didn't have a job like regular people do—I mean a place of work to go to. But he spent all his time watching over Mrs. Cooney, which was itself a kind of full-time job.

You see, Mrs. Cooney was the kind of person who, long ago, would have gotten burned at the stake for being a witch. It wasn't so much her looks, although she was sort of haunted looking; it was her strange predictions, secret promises, and mysterious warnings. Most people in Berkeley Bend had stopped paying attention to her murmurings, so she didn't share things with them anymore. However, Pauly and I, being kids, were often treated to some of her visions. She thought we believed every word she said—and we did, to a point.

One time she told Pauly about a "bad wind that was coming." The wind turned out to be Hurricane Hazel. Most everyone had cellars that filled up with water, and shingles that were blown-off by the time word got round. But only Pauly knew that Mrs. Cooney had predicted the very day and the hour that old Hazel was going to hit.

There were other times, though, when Mrs. Cooney got "messages from the Pleiades" that were just plain confusing. The Pleiades were a bunch of stars that talked to her. One time she told the mayor that Town Hall was going to be struck by a fireball on Christmas Eve because the Pleiades had told her so—and the mayor believed her. Well, that sure spoiled the volunteer firemen's Christmas, since they were all doing double duty; but no such thing ever happened. That lowered Mrs. Cooney's believability quite a bit. So, you see, with her you never knew what was genuine and what was a bunch of made-up junk. It wasn't easy to tell, partly because she made everything seem so definite and real.

She had these eyes, very large and round (one was slightly larger than the other), and when they lighted on you there was hell to pay, because then she really had you. I'm not saying she was a hypnotist or anything, but she had staring-power to beat the band, as she herself might say.

Otherwise she was nice looking and she held herself straight as a tree, and when she walked she was graceful and youthful, but I think she was actually in her sixties, the same age as her husband, who, as I said earlier, looked like Kendrick. Mrs. Cooney had the palest skin, kind of mushroomlike if you ask me, because she never went out in the sun, claiming that such bright light "quailed the face." She'd rather, she once said, go out at night and get a "moon tan," whatever that was.

What I was saying about the way she could look into your eyes: That was almost scary sometimes. Pauly was like an open book to her; she could tell him, any day of the week, just what he was thinking. I don't think she was ever wrong about that, either. Once, she said, in that cat's purr voice of hers, "Pauly, I believe you're feeling low today because of something to do with your sister."

Pauly eyed her edgily. "So why would I feel bad about Betty?"

"I don't mean Betty; I'm thinking of Judith," Mrs. Cooney said.

"Well, what about her?" Pauly said with his guard up.

Mrs. Cooney said wispily, "Something about a car, I think."

That was it. Bingo.

Pauly really clammed up.

Mrs. Cooney was amazing that way—she could find out anything she wanted. Pauly's eyes were like open windows, and all she had to do was look into them. However, I never saw her use these discoveries against anyone—unless, by chance, it was her husband. But I'm not sure she even did that. She was so very kindhearted.

I lived across the street from the Cooneys and I knew them pretty well, but like I said, most folks thought they were more than a little screwy, so they left them entirely alone. I don't know if Mrs. Cooney was aware of it, but a lot of the kids called her Cooney the Loony. I think she must have sensed something of the kind, because she was always imagining that people didn't like her, especially kids, and that they were up to no good, which was why she kept Kendrick.

The dog, that is.

Well, come to think of it, maybe she kept Kendrick the husband around for the same reason.

But then she was always up to something, some little skit or drama, it seemed to me, that had Mr. Cooney continually on his toes.

I remember the day when he went to the post office, and by the time he got back she'd put most of their furniture out on the front lawn and was preparing to have a yard sale.

"How could one teeny, tiny, little old woman move such a massive amount of furniture?" Mr. Cooney said to me when he saw what had happened. He was scratching his head and blinking his eyes in surprise. Which was saying a lot, because nothing much surprised him anymore. I suppose he'd seen it all. Pauly and I were hired, right on the spot, to help him move everything back inside where it belonged. And, you know, Mrs. Cooney showed us exactly where to put each and every article of furniture, and acted as if nothing had happened; we were, all of us, just doing a job that had to be done. But to this day I still don't understand how all that heavy junk got out there on their lawn. . . .

Now, every once and a while Mrs. Cooney would look me in the eye and ask if I knew when their house was going to burn down. Well, I didn't know what to say to that one. She had a thing with fire, I guess.

I would kind of shrug; I don't really remember.

After a time she was always asking this same question: "Do you know when the house is going to burn down?"

She would kind of angle her head in an odd way, and her eyes would narrow some—which was hard for her to do, since her left eye, which was slightly larger than her right one, was always beaming at you. So when she'd asked me the same dumb question five or ten times, I popped up with a good answer. I began saying, "I don't know, do you?" That usually works with folks who pester you with questions. I use it on my mom a lot.

But Mrs. Cooney would just let out a long sigh, and say, "We'll know soon enough."

Which made me wonder . . .

Sometimes I felt sorry for Mr. Cooney, though. Naturally, he had to live with her and put up with that stuff all the time. Pauly and I always wondered what he thought about things, but he seldom said what he felt; just what had to be done. Perhaps that was because Mrs. Cooney was always catching him up with something he didn't—and couldn't—expect. He used to tell us at least once a day: "Well, boys, I just have one bit of advice. Expect the worst, hope for the best." That was how he got along with her, I guess.

One day, however, he got really serious, and said: "Don't do anything she tells you to." He was coming in with the mail as we were returning with the dog.

"Now, see for yourself, boys." He took us into the kitchen—I don't know where Mrs. Cooney was at the time—and showed us all these shelves jammed full of catsup bottles. There must've been a couple hundred of them packed in there.

"Why would anyone want so many catsups?" Pauly said, wrinkling his nose and shaking his head.

Mr. Cooney cleared his throat, dropped his eyes. "I don't know," he said. "Maybe someone does, but I'm afraid I don't."

"Why don't you take them all back to O'Connor's Market?" I asked Mr. Cooney.

His lips tightened. "She'd know the moment I took them out of here."

"She didn't care when we moved back all the furniture," Pauly put in.

"That was different," Mr. Cooney said.

"How?" Pauly asked. He liked things straight and clear; indefiniteness drove him crazy. I suppose Mrs. Cooney was a bit more than Pauly could bear, but then Mr. Cooney seemed to be in the same muddle himself.

Now Mr. Cooney had a faraway look in his eyes, as if he could see something that we couldn't. "No, boys," he said softly, "the furniture was one thing and the catsups are another. Don't you see, I can't do anything that would hurt Mrs. Cooney's feelings. She loves those catsups, and while there's too many stored away to use in our lifetime, I can't . . . I just can't take them back."

I remembered, then, something she'd once said to me about the world coming to an end. She seemed to think it would; and perhaps in the not-too-distant future. Maybe the catsup bottles were her way of preparing for the end of the world. On the other hand, knowing Mrs. Cooney, she probably just liked the way they looked, like bottles of blood.

"Well, boys," Mr. Cooney said. "Just remember, if anything happens over here and I'm away, hang tight and stall for time."

In the case of the world's end, I wondered how much time we might have to stall, but as usual I didn't say anything. Sometimes it was hard for Pauly and me to tell which side of the fence we were really on. Being friends with Mrs. Cooney meant, in a way, betraying Mr. Cooney. Because everything she said and did seemed to make him nervous.

Later on that day, we were sitting on my lawn, looking out across at the Cooney's split-rail fence, just like the kind that Abe Lincoln made in Illinois before he became president. "Remember the day," I said to Pauly, "that she thought we were uprooting her fence?"

He laughed and rolled over in the grass, holding his belly.

"It's just like a Charlie Chan mystery—nobody knows what anybody else is doing, and everybody's guilty until proven innocent."

"Nobody ever touched that fence," I said, sucking on a grass stem. "Mrs. Cooney made that up, like she makes up most things."

"So you don't think the house is going to burn down?"

I shrugged. "Maybe I do, maybe I don't."

The truth was, I really didn't know. Pauly was right, it was just like Charlie Chan. "Remember the one called *The House Without a Key,* where the guy is found with a knife—"

"—in his heart and the trail of blood on his chest is made by a running lizard?" Pauly added, grinning.

Our favorite pastime was sitting up in my attic bedroom, which was also a kind of storage vault for my family's old stuff—my dad's 1930s Havana suits made of linen; my mom's pictures of dinosaurs with the Day-Glo eyes painted on cardboard packing crates; the piles of dusty phonograph records like Woody Herman hits, Hank Williams's "Luke the Drifter," "Tubby the Tuba" with the voice of Danny Kaye, old 78's of "The Blue Danube Waltz" and "The Peanut Vendor."

We'd sit up there all day, if we could get away with it,

watching my dad's discarded TV, the one with the six-inch square screen and the mahogany tube box surrounding it that was three feet high and weighed two hundred pounds. The only way you could see all the features in Charlie Chan, like how his eyes didn't slant a bit, was to hold a magnifying glass against the screen—the image was that small—and Pauly and I took turns holding it up and looking.

A couple days after this, when Pauly and I had taken Kendrick for his gallop around the woods and we were waiting for Mrs. Cooney to find us our fifty cents—half for me and half for Pauly—she said, "Oh, let me just give you a dollar, and you can apply it to next time."

Pauly said, "It's too much." But she came up so close, we could smell the rouge on her cheeks—they were red as apples—and said in a funny small voice, "If you can catch spiders, you can keep the change and apply it to yourselves."

"Spiders?" Pauly chirped.

I remembered what Mr. Cooney had told us about stalling for time if anything unusual were to come up, and this seemed a bit unusual, so I nudged Pauly with my elbow, as a little reminder.

Mrs. Cooney sort of encircled us with her large eye. I looked fondly at the back door, but it seemed, just then, a long ways off.

"Would you," she said, her voice brimming with secrets, "like to come under the table with me for a moment?" She gestured toward the kitchen table.

What a strange development this is, I thought. But at least it's under the Cooney roof, and Mr. Cooney will be back any minute, so maybe this could be called a stalling maneuver.

Anyway, she beckoned us with her large eye and her slightly smaller one, and then she got down on her knees, and lifting up the tablecloth, she crawled under the kitchen table.

Pauly went outside and waited on the porch, in case she should suddenly try and make a break for it. Either that, or he was scared of getting under the table with her—you know, since she had powers and all. That left me.

Well, I slid under the table quick as a cat. She had her legs folded under her Indian-style, as if she did this every hour on the hour.

"I don't want Mr. Cooney to know that I've got a great big black-and-yellow spotted salamander," she announced once we were both fully hidden by the tablecloth.

"You don't?"

"No, I positively don't."

She paused, her big eye searching around. "You won't tell him, will you?" She leaned close; I smelled rouge.

I told her I'd keep my mouth shut, and then I heard Pauly whistle outside. So I slid from under the table and headed outdoors.

"Get me some nice fat spiders," she called after me, "of the furry variety. And whatever you do, don't tell Mr. Cooney. You won't tell, will you?"

I scrambled out of there, promising her the moon while heading for the bright sunshine.

"Not so fast," she said stiffly, catching at my collar. "Do we have a deal, or don't we?"

I hate to be pinned down. I don't mind lying for the right reason, but I hate to be pressured into something I haven't bargained for. Besides, we already had a deal with Mr. Cooney. How could we have one with her, too?

I said, "Why can't I tell Mr. Cooney?"

She said, "We wouldn't want to hurt his feelings now, would we?"

"No," I softened, "we wouldn't want to do that."

But it sounded a lot like a trick to me. On the other hand, who was to say Mr. Cooney wasn't pulling some kind of trick of his own? The whole business was so mixed up, I didn't know whom to trust.

Later on, while walking the woods with Pauly, we talked about what would happen if Mr. Cooney found out. "The same as if she finds out about him telling us to keep an eye on her until he gets there," I remarked. "Anyway, what's the diff?"

Pauly pursed his lips, and nodded. "Peas in a pod," he said.

"What?"

"That's what my dad says. He says they're both nuttier than fruitcakes."

"Mr. Cooney too?"

Pauly nodded.

That day we dug around in the weeds and came up with a bunch of fat, furry spiders. These went direct to Mrs. Cooney (Mr. Cooney still wasn't back from the post office, which was pretty suspicious, if you ask me). We gave them to her in a number-four mason jar that we'd stuffed into a paper bag.

She met us at the door. I looked over my shoulder, expecting Mr. Cooney to come along.

"Isn't this nice?" she said, staring into the paper bag with intense pleasure. Then she placed it on the kitchen counter and went away, reappearing a moment later with a shoe box.

We watched in silence as she opened it up. Inside, on a mat of dead grass, was a black-and-yellow spotted salamander. The thing was about six inches long and thicker than a squash.

"Wow! He's really big!" Pauly exclaimed.

"Has to be," she said. Then, dreamily: "You know, to put out the fire."

"What fire?" I asked.

"The fire I told you about. . . . Don't you remember?"

"You mean the one that's going to burn down the house?" Pauly asked.

"That's the one," she confirmed, smacking her lips. Her big eye bulged, and brightened.

She continued: "I have told Mr. Cooney, oh, I don't know how many times . . . just doesn't seem to care; doesn't concern him one iota."

I was wondering what an iota was when she said: "You see, boys, I have had a dream."

We could tell she wasn't making that up by the way her eye started that sinking business again.

She continued gravely: "This dream was presented to me by the Elder Cedars of Lebanon."

"The what?" Pauly broke in.

"The ancient trees that live by our bedroom window," she said with certainty.

"Do they talk to you, Mrs. Cooney?" Pauly asked, showing that he was more than a little ill at ease with the subject.

I just kept staring at that granddaddy salamander. It looked like it was made out of molasses, but its hands—I swear, they were five-fingered and looked just like a baby's.

Mrs. Cooney pressed her lips into a thin line. Her eye rolled on the high seas a time or two. Then she said, very casual and ho-hum: "The day that the house burns, Mr. Cooney is going to take me for a motorcycle ride." At this her voice rose an octave, and she sounded pleased as punch, as if all her life she'd been waiting for that very moment to happen.

"Seven fire trucks—like the seven angels in Revelation."

"But this house is made out of stone," Pauly objected, adding, in the serene tone his father used: "Stone doesn't burn, Mrs. Cooney."

"All things burn . . . at the proper temperature," she said. Then her large eye closed, and the other one half closed, flickering. She spoke breathily: "The only thing that quenches a burning stone—is this!"

She thrust the shoe box at us. Automatically we both backed up. The spotted salamander wriggled once, proving that it was alive. Its puffy little fat kid's hands made as if to crawl up the side of the box. I got a good look at its shoe-button eyes just before she put the lid on the box and Mr. Cooney came up the driveway in his 1953 wood-paneled Chevrolet station wagon.

The car stopped, the emergency brake squawked, and he got out and shuffled up the walkway.

Mrs. Cooney withdrew into the shadowy interior of the fieldstone house.

"Everything all right, boys?" Mr. Cooney asked as he whistled up the walk.

We put on our freshest expressions of innocence.

He scratched his head, rubbed his chin.

"Watching over things . . . were you?" he asked.

And there we were—caught between the two of them. We'd known this was bound to happen sooner or later.

"Now, tell me the truth, boys," Mr. Cooney continued in his sandpapery voice. "Is Mrs. Cooney . . . acting up? Any signs of anything unusual?"

Neither Pauly nor I said a word. We looked off at Kendrick, who was barking at a bird.

"Something's astir, isn't it?" Mr. Cooney remarked knowingly.

We shrugged, our eyes resting on Kendrick.

I looked back at the house just as the wind made a rush at the Elder Cedars of Lebanon. I watched them as they leaned closer and closer to the house. Three wizened old wizards with bluish capes and conical blue hats.

Pauly started down the steps, mumbling: "She thinks the house is going to burn down and he's going to take her for a ride on a motorcycle which he doesn't have, and seven fire trucks, or angels—or whatever—are going to come and—oh, I'm heading home!"

"Mugumblefarble!" I shouted. It was our secret word, the

one that meant all things at once: *hello/good-bye/pleasant dreams/look at that girl/ don't say a word until we meet again . . .*

So it was that Pauly and I had shifted sides. We'd mutinied, signed up, sort of, with Mrs. Cooney. All along, you see, we had humored her and secretly worked for him. Now it was the other way around: We were humoring him and working for her. Even Charlie Chan would've chuckled over this turn of events. Or his Number One Son might've said: "Hey, Pop, what's up is down."

There was nothing we could do about it now, either.

The next day, as we were walking Kendrick, Mr. Cooney came over to us and said, "Boys, that malarkey about the house-a-fire and the seven trucks, and the motorcycle madness and all the rest of it, well, it's really nothing."

"It's something to me," I said.

"Me too," Pauly said.

"Pooh!" Mr. Cooney said. He brushed a bit of dust off his windbreaker, went inside the house, and closed the door behind him. I noticed that his shoulders looked tight and square, and he didn't bother to say good-bye.

After that, he didn't confide in us again. He pretty much ignored us, as we did him. We still took Kendrick for his gallops every day and caught spiders for Mrs. Cooney, but we stayed away from Mr. Cooney; and he stayed away from us, as well.

Then it happened. I woke up one summer night and the fire engines were wailing. Jumped out of bed, ran to the open window, and for a second I thought I was dreaming. There it was, just as she'd said: the fieldstone house in flames.

There were four fire trucks lined up on the lawn already, and more coming up all the time. It wasn't long before seven trucks had surrounded the house; there were trucks from Warren Township, and Newton, and everywhere else.

Mr. Cooney was out on the lawn, in his pajamas, directing the firemen with their black-slick coats and snout-nosed fire hoses. Mrs. Cooney had Kendrick on his leash, and he was galloping in place, pawing a hole in the ground. I wondered how such a small woman could hold on to such a big dog. But then size doesn't really count in cases like this, does it?

She also had something under her arm; and though I couldn't see all that well, with the flashing lights and the confusion and everything, it seemed to me the thing under her left arm was a shoe box.

An ocean of water was pouring into every window of the Cooney house, and the flames were licking around the roof like orange snakes.

I had a kind of grandstand seat for the event, the flat roof off the second-story window of our house, and I could see it all just as it happened.

After a while their roof exploded, sending crisp tails of spark and smoke into the starless sky. After that, the stone shell of the Cooney house was all that was left, and the firemen trained their hoses into the open roof, and they sent a ton of water in there. I bet they drained the Watchung Reservoir before the blaze was out altogether.

After a time, Pauly showed up in my yard, rubbing the smoke out of his eyes. "My mom wouldn't let me come until it was put out," he said crossly. My parents were watching the whole thing from their window and keeping an eye on me at the same time, so I hadn't missed a trick.

I asked if I could go down and meet Pauly on our lawn, and my dad said yes but my mom said no. But since Pauly was there anyway and the fire was almost out, she finally gave in and I went down in my pj's, and we took in the last of the smoking and talking and the end-of-the-fire hose-squirting.

Then Mr. Cooney wheeled a motorcycle out of nowhere, and as Mrs. Cooney restrained Kendrick, he kick-started it, and got it grumbling and going.

We watched as he rumbled up the driveway, weaving weirdly in between the fire trucks, and saying something nice to each of the soot-blackened firemen.

"I didn't know he could ride one of those things!" Pauly said.

"I didn't know he had one," I said.

"We should've known," Pauly added.

"Yeah," I said.

"Now, boys," Mr. Cooney called over the growling motorcycle.

We went over to him, admiring the glittery chrome and steel, the sparkly paint on the monster-tired motorcycle that was every kid's dream of flying close to the earth without wings.

"Would you be kind enough to watch Kendrick for a spell?" Mr. Cooney asked pleasantly, as if nothing out of the ordinary was taking place. "Just for a little while, until I get

Mrs. Cooney settled for the night," he put in apologetically.

"Sure," I offered. "I'll take him up to my room."

"But where are you going to go now?" Pauly wondered.

"Oh, just down to the Nightlighter," he gestured, as if riding motorcycles and lodging in motels was what he always did on summer nights after his house burned down.

And then, above the gargling of the bike's motor and the backing up of the fire engines, he said to us, with that superconfidential smile: "Let's just keep this between ourselves, shall we, boys?"

"What?" Pauly asked, dumbfounded.

"Let's keep this whole affair to ourselves," Mr. Cooney requested.

I said, "You mean the motorcycle?"

He said, "I mean the fire."

"The fire?" Pauly squeaked.

"You know, boys," he admitted, "sometimes she's right and sometimes she's wrong. But she's really hell to live with when she's right. Get what I mean?"

We said we did, but I still don't, and Pauly doesn't either.

Maybe Charlie Chan could figure it out, but we couldn't, or wouldn't. One thing was sure, though, Mr. and Mrs. Cooney were, somehow, made for each other. One without the other would've been like lemonade without sugar, or a hot dog without the bun.

A little while later Mrs. Cooney came out of the crowd and the confusion. She had the crumpled shoe box under her left arm, and she straddled the seat behind Mr. Cooney, and they both scuttled off through the steam and the smoke, heading toward the Nightlighter Motel in downtown Berkeley Bend. I could've sworn I saw them smiling, but Pauly said they were grimacing from the smoke.

And that was just about the last we ever saw of them. The next morning, Mr. Cooney came in a rental car to pick up Kendrick. He gave me a crisp twenty-dollar bill, patted me on the back, and said, "Remember our deal. If you should ever see Mrs. Cooney privately, please don't mention anything to her about the fire. It would only hurt her feelings."

A few days later the Cooneys left Berkeley Bend. We never saw them, or Kendrick, ever again. Some people said the fire was a hoax and some said arson and others pointed out there would be a big investigation before it was over; but nothing ever happened. The fire inspector concluded along with the insurance company that the fire got started on account of summer lightning.

What was left of the only fieldstone house in Berkeley Bend was bulldozed. A sign in the yard said: LOT FOR SALE. But no one ever bought it. No one even bothered to look at it, as far as I knew.

I used to go over there with Pauly and we'd snoop around the old fire-blackened stones. There wasn't much there, though. Just the foundation of the house, which, that summer, after heavy rain, filled up and turned into a scummy pond. Strangely enough, that clotted water never seeped away. It stayed there like a black mirror burning darkly in the sun. And once, when I was staring at my reflection, I saw something crawling in that silver-black glare. At first I thought it was just my imagination, but I kept staring, and then I knew what it was. Yes, it had to be; couldn't be anything else.

Out of the murky bottom crawled a great black-and-yellow spotted salamander, the kind that has baby hands and shoe-button eyes.

Cindy, Ally, Wally and Buzz, and the Gang

I work at Doctor Moledinky's Animal Museum on weekends; how I got the job is another story, which I'll tell about later. But anyway, I always hand-feed Cindy, the coatimundi—no one else can get near her, not even Dr. Moledinky.

The museum's cages are outdoors. They're just big bird-cages, most of them. Open to the rain and sun, so people can stroll along and see the monkey, the alligator, the bobcat, the john crow, the coatimundi, and such.

The high point of everybody's day is when Pauly and I feed the animals their midday meal.

We have to mix up a different preparation of food for each one—sixty animals in all.

We give Allywumpus, the alligator, a portion of raw meat and fish dipped in cod-liver oil. I stand on the edge of the tank and toss it in. Ally's pretty tolerant when it comes to cage entry, but I don't as a rule hang around in there.

Feeding Ally goes something like this:

Toss—

Clack!

Meatfishandsometimespoultry—

Gone!

There is no real danger, however, unless you stand in the water with her, which naturally I never do. She's an efficient eater, though, I can tell you that. Fortunately she waits her turn until I make my toss. Otherwise it could get pretty hairy in there.

I guess it's a game with old Ally. She really wants to show folks that she can still catch meat on the wing by hardly moving anything except her upper jaw. I don't know how old she is, but Dr. Moledinky once told me when he bought her some years back at a Florida gator farm, she was sixty-something.

Cindy, the coatimundi (Dr. Moledinky calls her a ringtail cat), is the all-round gentlest animal in the whole museum. Not to everyone, though. Dr. Moledinky can't get near Cindy. You see, generally she prefers men to women, but with Dr. Moledinky she makes an exception—I really don't know why. Unless it's because his hands always smell like fountain-pen ink. Animals are funny that way. Certain smells make them go haywire.

Anyway, she really despises women of any age at all, even little girls.

They always stand back after I tell them her disposition toward them, as if they had such a feeling already, just being near the cage, and watching Cindy pace like a cross between a cat and a monkey. She's a mammal, by the way, a little bigger than a good-sized cat, related to the raccoon. Her fur is thick and soft and well groomed, and she is very light and delicate on her feet.

I hand-feed Cindy. She eats a mixture of diced-up tropical fruit. After I get inside her cage, I dip my hand into the larder pail. Very politely, Cindy comes mincing over to me with her delicate little hand-feet, her ring tail up high and curled slightly back, and that face with the thin black mask and the long, sensitive, ever-sniffing snout.

I love Cindy, and she knows it.

She comes over and puts her hands on my knees. Then she sniffs me all over with her soft, slender nose, to see where I've been that day.

If she likes where I've been—it's that simple!—she raises her snout and sings for her supper. (Coatis make a soft, small, high-pitched purring noise when they're happy.) Then I kneel down and offer her slices of peach and pineapple. (Coatis eat real garbage, if you give it to them, but we don't—and wouldn't.) She loves fresh fruit, chewing it carefully with her sharp little cat's teeth. But Cindy's never, ever, not even once, nipped me.

However, if Dr. Moledinky or some lady comes over to her cage, she growls like a miniature cougar.

It's hard to feed the animals in any kind of normal way because there are so many people standing around watching. That's why the animals are usually grumpy and have bad eating habits.

They really want to be left alone when they eat, but it's not possible at Doctor Moledinky's Animal Museum.

My worst, and most dangerous, animal is the mean little

greedy groundhog named Wally, who's always, rain or shine, baring his fangs and diving for my ankle.

No matter what, the moment Wally sees leg—any leg—he wants to bite it. So now Pauly, who was his feeder, won't go near.

He came out that first day with the toe of his sneaker torn off—and after that, I was elected by Dr. Moledinky to feed Wally myself. Only he did say, "Get a pair of boots, son."

Oh, those teeth of Wally's. They are bright and sharp, and the color of caramel corn.

Whew!

That's why I always carry a small U.S. Army camp shovel to ward Wally off me.

To make matters worse, Wally's bunkmate is a Jamaican john crow buzzard. Okay, Wally lives underground, but Buzz, as we call her, perches on the barkless branch just over the entrance of the cage.

The moment I go into that cage, Wally chitters like a rattler at mating season and dives for my ankle. Same time, Buzz starts whamming me on the head with her three-foot wings.

You can get bruised by a buzzard's wing, let me tell you!

There are some high old times in Wally and Buzz's quarters. Once I forgot my Army shovel, and I had to dance fast to get out of there in one piece.

The charging groundhog is relentless. This always makes the crowd roar with laughter.

What a show!

They shriek, they howl—yes, like animals!

But if they only knew what I know—that Wally is a killer with no conscience—I bet they would not carry on with so much enthusiasm. On the other hand, maybe they would.

Buzz is almost as wicked, in her own way, as Wally is aggressive. She hangs on to her branch and beats you silly.

You have to dodge her, see her coming and going, or you'll get knocked onto your can—a deadly setup for the chittery jaws of Wally.

Going in, I dance about, feinting from side to side and moving up and down, taking care not to drop the two feed pails; one of grain, one of rotted meat. You see, my hands are full, so I have to be extra careful. I have the two pails, plus the Army shovel under my arm. To survive Wally and Buzz at the same time, I have to be very fast and sure: Get in, drop pails, be ready with shovel, look out for overhead wing-tremors. You just can't walk in there, ho-hum and lackadaisical, and expect to get out alive.

As added protection against Wally, I wear these huge old engineer's boots. He could bite through them only if I was knocked out by one of Buzz's hard right hooks.

Dr. Moledinky offers me his African pith helmet for head protection against Buzz. But to tell you the truth, I don't think it's given out of kindness.

I think he likes to see me wear it in there because Buzz always knocks it off my head. And that's one more thing I have to worry about—so I'm not wearing the hat anymore, thanks.

I know Dr. Moledinky likes to see me skirmishing in the

cages because it's good for business. You should see the people line up at feeding time.

Waiting for the Wally, Buzz, and Andy Show to begin.

Now, every day or so, Tom Sola comes to the museum and loans Dr. Moledinky a squirrel or a tame blue jay, and once he even brought in a small brown, leather-winged bat, but it wasn't tame. Tom lives on the outer edge of Berkeley Bend, he's a loner whose main thing in life is animals: watching them, talking to them, tracking them, and catching them.

His job at the museum is taking care of his pet crow; he's sort of given it to the museum on a permanent loan. The crow's name is Sandy, and on a good day she'll talk pretty to a stranger. But you should hear her talk to Tom. He's got some way with animals. I've asked him to teach me some of the things he knows, but most of it isn't something you can pick up in a day or two. Like, for instance, the way he walks, slow and soft-footed, so you can hardly hear him coming or going. Animals trust Tom and I suppose that's why Dr. Moledinky likes to have him around.

The most amazing thing is how quickly he can calm a creature down. I've seen our marmoset monkey, the one named Tetra that you could put in a sugar bowl, dancing around madly, begging for food. Tom comes along, padding silently, and he presses his lips together and makes a high-pitched squeak, and suddenly Tetra's quiet as a mouse.

I don't know how he does it, but if I can, I'm going to learn. Because that's why I took this job in the first place. One day, in addition to being a writer, I want to have an animal farm, only my animals, I promise, won't be in cages. They'll just hang around the house and come and go as they please, like people.

Cages, I think, make creatures crazy.

But I am learning a lot, working at the museum.

After a while, when you're with animals all the time, you start to really see how they see things—that is, nosewise. You start to smell a bit more, check around before you do something dumb. We say animals aren't as smart as people, but I believe they are actually smarter, only in different ways.

I have heard Sandy making fun of a lady's hat and, at the same time, wishing she had pieces of it to store in her nest. And I've seen Cindy give a darting glance to someone who called her a monkey, or a cat—she seems to know when people don't know what she is. One thing's for sure: All of the animals at the museum have an opinion about what people are, and mostly, I think, it's not complimentary.

So I guess I am beginning to talk to animals—their own way. And I imagine that if I only knew the right words, I could give Wally a piece of my mind instead of accidentally offering him a piece of my flesh.

Tom, Caller of Crows

Tom Sola lived in the only house at the end of Drift Road. Well, it wasn't much of a house; a tiny cottage was more like it. And Drift Road was hardly much of a road; a cow path was more like it. The kids at school used to call him the "dumb drift of Drift Road." I guess Pauly and I were his only friends.

To get to Tom's, you went down to the red-brick Lutheran Church on the corner of Emerson and Plainfield—this was just a block or two from my house; then back of the cemetery and up a ways, and there, kind of sketchy looking under all those shade trees, was Drift Road.

The forest gets thick after you make the turn; white birch, blue spruce, and cedar. And so quiet that, as Tom used to say, "you can hear the grass whispering and the leaves growing. . . ." Or was it the other way around?

We met Tom one hot day just about sundown when Pauly and I were looking for a new swimming hole. We were poking around the edge of the old cemetery, reading gravestones, when we heard some running water, maybe a waterfall. A few feet into the woods, just off from the cemetery, we saw what appeared to be a small creek. We followed it for a while until it went off a little cliff.

Now, Pauly and I were about to climb down there and go for a swim when we saw a big black crow come down through the trees, cawing.

And then we heard more of the same—crow cawing—just behind us coming from the other direction. We turned around, and there was this long lanky fellow with a great jutting jaw like a muskellunge fish and Huck Finn hair, mostly hanging in his eyes, and an expression on his face that was a cross between gloom and despair.

Well, he was walking along, making great strides through the spaces between the trees, and every now and then he flung back his head and you could see his Adam's apple bob, and then he'd let out a long, loud crow call that shattered the blue sky and made us shiver right down to our bones, because it was eerie hearing a human being make such a sound.

Pauly asked, "Isn't that the guy who catches animals for Dr. Moledinky?"

"Yeah. He goes to our school," I said, "but he cuts a lot. No one ever talks to him, and he doesn't talk to them, either."

"I can see why, if he just does bird-talk."

The two of us watched as several crows appeared out of nowhere and followed the crow caller downhill toward the river.

"Let's watch," Pauly said.

We sat down on a fallen hickory tree and watched. Down

by the river he stripped off his clothes and jumped into the sink hole there. A bunch of crows were circling around him, skimming near the water. From where we were sitting, they were like pieces of sooty paper, blowing around the white rocks.

Then he put his hands to his mouth and he hooted like a barred owl. He barked and boomed and even made a kind of screaming noise. Since it was beginning to grow dark, the crows fell away into the cracks of the trees, looking for a safe place to roost.

"Did you see that?" Pauly exclaimed. "He made the crows go away. That guy's like Daniel Boone, or something!"

"I could do that," I said, feeling about one inch tall.

"You wish you could do that," he said, knowing I couldn't.

"Well, all right, I wish I could," I said, knowing he was right.

"Let's go down and meet him," Pauly ventured.

And we did.

And that was how we got to know Tom, the crow caller, the kid the others called "the drift of Drift Road."

He was special, Tom was; we knew that right away. The way he made friends with us, for example. That day we met him, he asked us right off if we'd ever gone hand-fishing. Pauly said nope, and so did I.

"Well, I don't think I could ever be friends with guys that couldn't ketch a leetle feesh in their hand," Tom teased, winking at both of us.

He talked funny, but you could see he was serious.

"I can do it," I boasted.

"Cannot," Pauly prattled.

"How 'bout I show you," Tom said.

That was how we got to be friends: by rolling up our sleeves and hanging over a rock ledge and waiting for fish to come along, and then—*whiz-zap!*—lighting onto them. Only, to be honest, we—Pauly and I—didn't whiz-zap them that much; in fact, hardly at all. Well, to be perfectly bald about it—not at all.

But Tom didn't care; he just liked showing us things, and he was always very good-humored. And even though he was older than we were (by a couple years), it didn't matter since he never brought it up or made you feel any less for it.

Tom was funny and wise, and he knew a lot of things that nobody else knew, especially about animals. He talked as if the words were mush in his mouth and his voice sounded like an old man's and he had the strangest accent you ever heard: a cross between hillbilly and Spanish, or something. His vocal chords didn't work all that well either—they'd make creaking sounds and he'd suddenly talk very loud.

I asked him once, when he was talking loud that way, if he thought I was deaf. He said, "No, sir, I am."

I figured he was just kidding, but he wasn't.

"Didn't I ever tell you I was deaf?" he asked me later, after we got to know him.

I said, "Uh-uh."

He saw my curiosity, and maybe my disbelief.

He replied, "I was born like that, mostly deaf. Had to learn words the hard way, reading lips. Sounds I hear just fine—there's a difference."

"You do a darn good job," Pauly told him.

Tom snorted. He always snorted when he didn't want to talk. And that closed things off, shut the conversation down. It was obvious to me he heard things in a different way than the rest of us.

Another time I asked him where his mother was, because we'd met his father and his brother, but we had never seen his mother.

"Mama . . ." Tom said thickly, and clamped up.

A hank of hair hung down over his eyes. He disappeared behind it when he didn't want to talk. Then he wouldn't come out until he was good and ready.

This particular time we were calling a cowbird away from a robin's nest. Tom didn't like the way cowbirds stole robins' eggs, so he used to make the mating call and draw them away. We were sitting in some heavy cover, swatting mosquitoes.

And Tom stayed undercover, with his long black hair hanging down, not saying anything. Finally he opened his mouth, and the words came out slow as winter honey.

"My mama died when I was leetle," Tom said, looking vaguely into the leaves. "I never knew her. My brother, Stan, was the one who raised me."

Now Pauly and I knew Stan just a little bit—no one in Berkeley Bend knew him very well. Stan wore expensive clothes, and he drove a '56 Chevy station wagon with a 382-horsepower engine with a four-barrel carburetor and duel-manifold exhaust. It was a fast car, and when Drift Road was boiling dust, you could be sure it was Stan. And when there was a fight somewhere, it was usually Stan. He kept a dog chain in his back pocket for such events. But when it came to taking care of Tom, it was Stan, too. I can tell you that nobody watched over a brother like Stan Sola watched over Tom; like a chicken hawk he was, taking in every little angle.

"You know my dad," Tom said. He whistled a cowbird call, then pushed the hair out of his eyes.

"I've talked to him a couple times," I said.

"He's a drunk," Tom said matter-of-factly.

He whistled again, and a grayish bird flew over our heads, making icy little cheeps.

"Drunk or not . . . he's all I got . . . or will ever get," Tom said.

I remembered the first time I saw his dad, sitting in a handmade cedar chair in a grove of birches. He hardly moved. You would know he was there only because of the darkness in the flickering leaves, a darkness that even the sun couldn't erase with its rays.

"He sure don't amount to much," Tom added, getting up to go. He rubbed around his eyes and snorted deeply.

Pauly said, "Stan's kinda like a mother and a brother and a father all rolled into one. You don't really need anyone else."

Tom didn't say anything. We were walking back to his house, passing under the white blaze of birches. The light of those trees brightened Tom's old-looking face and made him smile.

"If I ever think of being lonely . . . if it ever starts to make me feel low . . . you know, Stan's not around all that much . . . then I come here . . . these trees—"

That was all he said, but we understood.

We stood there in the light, the burning white bark all around us. The green bubble-shaped leaves patting at the blue sky.

Tom's cottage was two rooms with a screened-in porch and an outhouse. Inside, it was so small that the walls seemed to lean against you. It was dark in there; and very moldy. Unbreathable, if you ask me. The windows were always shut, even in summer. The glass was gray-blue, fly stained, and fogged. His dad always left a pile of Prince Albert tobacco cans on a stump out back, but he left empty jugs of Cribari wine all around, and you had to be careful not to trip on them.

I told Pauly the cottage smelled like a dog's rug that had been left out in the rain.

"That's weird," Pauly said.

"Why?"

"'Cause Tom doesn't have a dog."

"I mean, Pauly, it just smells like that."

But Pauly never did care for figurative language. He liked things spelled out, so I told him Tom's house stunk, and he agreed.

Then one day, out of the blue, Tom said, "You know, if we had a dog, I'd let him sleep on my bed with his head on my pillow."

Pauly said, "Are you sure you don't have a dog already?"

"No, but if I had one . . ."

Ever since I'd said the thing about the dog-rug smell, Pauly was sure Tom was holding out on us. He now thought the

Solas had a big wet dog tied up in the woods and they only let it in nights, when we weren't around.

Another time, we were tracking a possum up in back of Drift Road when Tom told me, "Possums don't hibernate like a lot of other animals. They're not much good in the cold."

"What do they do in the winter?" I wanted to know as we stepped over a mossy log.

Tom blew on his hands, as if remembering how cold the winter had been.

"Are you cold?"

Studying my lips, he shook his head: "Naw, but saying such, makes me feel such . . . know what I mean?"

Saying things like that in school got Tom the reputation of being daft or dumb. But Pauly and I loved the way he talked, his own special way of stringing his words.

"Looky here," Tom said with obvious pleasure.

There was a soft, fresh possum track in the dirt at our feet. You could see the possum's handprint very clearly.

Tom remarked, "The old hot road got some tar on his fingers. . . ."

"How do you know?" Pauly asked.

We looked closer at the print. Sure enough, there were some black dots where the pads had pressed into the earth.

Pauly bent down close, and sniffed.

"Tar all right," he confirmed.

Tom beamed. "Told ya."

"Then why'd he step in it? If he could've gone around, I

mean." Pauly wrinkled his nose and looked at Tom, who started to snort.

Then Tom said, "Possums aren't stupid, Pauly . . . but they're not what you'd call . . ."

Tom's face clouded.

He glanced at me. His serious black eyes were searching for something. His shag hair fell over them, screening him.

"See this?" Tom pointed at the print. "That's old possum's thumb. . . . He's got one, just like we do. Hard to figure, ain't it?"

"What's hard to figure, Tom?"

He shook his shag head.

"Possums being dumb," he retorted. "If they got that thumb, fer chrissakes, why don't they use it, like old racoon does? Once I seen a possum sitting in a wheel track of a winter's day . . . him wishing he could pull himself out of there. And he could've . . . if he'd only known he had a thumb!"

We had never heard Tom say so many words in a row. But then I'd never seen a possum print, either.

Pauly was staring at his thumb, measuring against the possum track. "Why is a thumb so all-fired important, Tom?" Pauly asked.

Tom smiled broadly. His eyes opened wide.

"Well, sir," he said importantly, "for one thing . . . thumbs are real good for raising and pulling yourself out of places you don't want to be. You ever try to lift yourself off a fence with no thumb, Pauly?"

Pauly shook his head.

"Let's go try," I said.

We walked back through the woods. There was a big stone fence around the red-brick Lutheran Church. Pauly and I tried to climb over it, with our thumbs tucked under our palm, but we couldn't do it; you just couldn't get a decent grip no matter how hard you tried.

Pauly lay back in the grass, laughing.

"See what you mean," he sputtered. "Thumb's just about everything, isn't it?"

"Can't talk without a tongue," Tom chuckled.

"Can't climb without a thumb," Pauly returned.

I asked, "If old possum's got one, then why doesn't he use it?"

"Whaat I want to know," Tom laughed.

Tom knew more about animals than anyone—even Dr. Moledinky. Tom used to bring in skunks, muskrats, possums, and squirrels, and he'd allow Dr. Moledinky to keep them for a while, usually just a day or two; then he'd take them back and let them loose. But after a while he wouldn't bring them in anymore.

I asked him why, and he said: "You know why—Moledinky'd rather have a squirrel floating in a bottle . . . than running up a tree." And he snorted with finality.

There came a day, though, when Dr. Moledinky wished he was on better terms with Tom. That was the day when he lost the diamond key chain for his 1947 Buick Dina-Flo sedan, the big green bullet-shaped automobile with acres of gleaming chrome up front that looked like shark's teeth, and more chrome along the sides. Inside, it was built like a houseboat, all butternut-wood paneled and cream carpeted, and the clock ticked loud enough to wake the dead.

Dr. Moledinky offered a hundred-dollar reward for anyone who could find that key ring.

Pauly and I went out hunting. I guess the whole town did. But nobody turned up anything.

"We've been up and down Mountain Avenue for days," Pauly complained. "And all we found was some Brooklyn Dodgers baseball cards."

"What about the two mounted bullets in the cedar box?" I reminded him.

"You got to keep them," Pauly countered.

"Only for the first week; then they're yours again."

Pauly said, "What we want's a nice little gold-and-silver chain with diamond studs on it. We find that, we get the reward!"

"Tom's the best tracker in Berkeley Bend," I pointed out. "Why don't we ask him to try and find it?"

"Think he'd split the reward?" Pauly wondered.

"Tom's not greedy," I said.

So we walked up Drift Road on a hot sunny day and paid a visit on Tom, who was making his own fishing lures.

Tom listened to our offer and grinned. He put the horsehair dry fly down on the bare birch stump he was working over, and scratched his chin.

"Why, I found a cute leetle diamond key chain the other day," Tom said brightly, his voice cracking.

"Where?" Pauly gasped.

"Somewhere," Tom said evasively. He had a funny look on his face, like a possum eating fox grapes.

Pauly and I looked at each other.

"That key chain's got a hundred-dollar reward tacked to it," I said to Tom.

"I know," he said hollowly.

"Are you—sure?" I questioned.

"Lookee here," Tom said. He reached into one of his pockets and produced two handfuls of junk. A piece of broken mirror, a busted-up Pez holder, a copper penny, and a lot of lint.

"Bunch of roadside trash," Tom smiled, his voice on the verge of cracking. "To some . . ." he added meaningfully.

"What about—to others?" Pauly asked.

Tom chuckled; his hair was flopped in front of his face as he picked up the fly and started tying it again. I watched his nimble fingers work the horsehair, tying it tightly; then he drew the knot together with his teeth.

He held the fly up to the sun.

The light filtered through the imaginary wings he'd created out of a twist of cellophane and wren's feather.

"Going to be a dancy one, this. . . ." Tom announced, pleased.

"What about the key chain?" I reminded him.

He said slowly, "Wouldn't it be funny . . . if some dumb hick by the name of Tom . . . that everybody makes fun of behind his back . . . wouldn't it be a laugh if he come up with the hundred-dollar key chain?"

Pauly looked at the pocket junk Tom had placed on the stump where he was working.

"What's this stuff got to do with it?" he questioned.

"There's a riddle," Tom said teasingly. "Who flaps his wings . . . and hides his things?"

"Sandy the crow," I exclaimed.

Tom cawed loudly. "First and best guess," he said, and thumped me on the back.

"Let's not forget how we first met," I told him.

"So, have you got it figured out?" Tom asked.

Pauly looked puzzled.

I said, "Don't you see, Pauly? Tom just went out and asked Sandy where the key chain was, and she told him."

Tom elbowed me with a grin. His face was brighter than I'd ever seen it before. "She told me where the good doctor dropped it . . . right in front of his very own '47 Buick—"

"And where she swooped down and picked it up and took it to her nest," I said, completing the puzzle.

Pauly raised his fists at the sky and yelled: "Tom, you're a genius!"

"Well, no," Tom said, suddenly embarrassed. "I'm not that."

I said, "You're just a smart old, two-thumbed, money-grabbing possum, that's all—and now we're rich!"

Tom grinned from ear to ear. "Now, isn't that the prettiest dry fly you ever saw tied end to end with a good-for-nothing piece of horse's tail?" he joked.

And that was the first time I ever heard Tom say a complete sentence without stopping twice in the middle. It was also the first time I ever heard him make a joke.

The following day Tom took us over to the Moledinky museum. It was after hours and the place was closed up for the night. An early quiet, made of shadows, had settled over the rows of empty-looking cages. I saw a gray fox dancing across the barren ground in front of its burrow. A sleepy buzzard straightened its wings against the fading sunlight and—I swear—yawned.

Tom showed Pauly and me the open area where Sandy the crow came and perched. "She's not here . . . most of the time," Tom said as he ducked under the perch. "Anyways . . . here's her nest."

"Doesn't she get mad if you go poking around in it?" Pauly asked.

"She don't care if I mess with her things . . . long as I put them back."

"You mean," I said, amazed, "that Sandy knows what she's got in there?"

"Every leetle item," Tom said as he reached into her great unruly pile of sticks and papers. "Lookee here," he cried, his voice crackling.

We watched as Tom brought Sandy's treasure over to where Pauly and I could see it. There was red and green Christmas tinsel; a white wooden golf tee; a tiny plastic ship-in-a-bottle; a pretty piece of amber sap, crystallized like hardened honey; a cat's-eye marble; a Straight Arrow decoder ring; a steel-gray baking-soda–powered miniature submarine; and the broken cone of a water-pressured space rocket.

"Look at all that stuff," Pauly said admiringly. "I didn't know crows were such collectors."

"That's all they do," Tom remarked. "Here's more." His eyes burned darkly, and he dipped his hand into Sandy's nest again and brought forth another handful of goodies. This time there were Nehi Orange bottle caps, a Mars Bar wrapper, a Bazooka Double Bubble Gum comic.

"Still no . . ." Pauly said doubtfully.

Tom dipped again. "Sandy told me," he mumbled, ". . . and Sandy never lies." His hand appeared with the last of the crow's piecemeal collectibles.

His fingers opened slowly: a Muriel cigar ring, a chunk of rose-colored bath tile, a brass pen holder and desk chain, and a diamond key chain.

Tom looked up at the sky and smiled.

"Told you," he chuckled softly.

Suddenly Dr. Moledinky came out of the dusky shadows and padded up behind Tom. "Soooo," he said, ironing the word on his tongue. "Find anything interesting in that crow's nest, Tom?"

Tom turned around and scratched his head.

"The good doctor." He grinned as if expecting him at that very moment.

Dr. Moledinky was not very tall, but he made up for it by being broad and rather square. He had a block head, heavy-rimmed eyeglasses, and a mustache that looked like a toothbrush pasted upon his upper lip.

"Caught you red-handed," Dr. Moledinky snapped.

The last bit of sun lanced through the hazy leaves of the maples and lit the diamond key chain so that first Dr. Moledinky and then Pauly and I saw it there, gleaming in Tom's outstretched hand.

And then something like a black bomb dropped down and snatched it up. It was Sandy, and she was cawing crazily, telling all human thieves where they could go.

"Why, you—" Dr. Moledinky roared, shaking his fist at the bird as she drifted off through the trees.

But already she was gone, back into the shadows.

We heard her cawing, *Thief, thief,* in the dark woods.

I glanced at Dr. Moledinky. He was about to come undone. He pounded his fist into his palm.

"I knew I never should have let that bird get the run of this place!" he said, glaring at Tom. Then, "It's all your fault, setting up that open-air exhibit."

Tom looked at him in that weightless way of his. But his voice didn't crack when he said, "You want your pretty leetle key chain, Doctor?"

Dr. Moledinky's face relaxed at once. He took Tom by the arm, as if they were suddenly partners again: "Find the crazy bird and I'll make good the reward," he said in a gravelly voice.

Tom blinked and moved one step away from him. Dr. Moledinky let go of his arm.

"She's got another tree," Tom said simply.

"Do you know where it is?" Dr. Moledinky asked.

Tom ignored the question. Looking at Pauly and me, he continued: "Crows don't like the dark . . . so she's heading for her other nest right now."

"Tom," Dr. Moledinky said, "I have to admire your cunning. Why, you must be half crow yourself."

Tom straightened up and looked at us once again: "Sandy's no thief. That chain, far as I can tell, belongs to her as much as it does to the good doctor here. After all," he reasoned, "she found it on the road, and in my book . . . well, finders keepers."

Dr. Moledinky, squaring himself off, appeared deep in thought. "You may have a point," he said, his arms folded squarely, his chin pulled in.

He paused, his chin jabbed forward, and he struck a dramatic pose. "I suppose we are all just borrowers at heart," he confided.

We said nothing. We just looked at Dr. Moledinky, who had begun pacing back and forth. "Tom, you're right," he said emphatically. Then his voice grew soft and coaxing. "Still and all, you think you might find it again?"

"Do you forgive Sandy?" Tom wanted to know.

"I forgive the whole world," Dr. Moledinky said, opening up his arms as if to embrace the empty air.

"All right," Tom said, suddenly relenting. "I'll get it back for you then."

"The money's yours if you get that key chain; and by god I'll double the reward and get a key chain for Sandy, too!"

"It's gotta look just like the original one," Tom said.

"Just so," Dr. Moledinky agreed. "Only I'll get a five-and-dime rhinestone instead of a real diamond."

Tom was hesitant. "Do they look the same?" he asked uncertainly.

Dr. Moledinky nodded.

"It'd take a jeweler's glass to tell the difference."

"All right," Tom said, "I figger it's settled."

He then moved off into the shadows like a cat, and the rest of us followed. After a little while we came to the hill where we had first met Tom. It was almost too dark to see. But against the white boil of the river, we were able to make out a twilight outline of a tall dead tree, which Tom explained was Sandy's second hideout.

"That's her winter retreat," Tom whispered. Then he descended into the gorge while Dr. Moledinky and Pauly and I waited; and watched.

Soon we heard a hooting and a cawing. A black shape came out of the dead tree and flapped windily over our heads, beating back the way we had come. Tom scrambled up the rise, grinning in the half-dark. He was holding the diamond key chain in his outstretched hand.

"Here," he said to Dr. Moledinky, "before I forget."

"Well, well," Dr. Moledinky said in a hushed voice. "You might as well know, Tom, that my wife, Lorraine, gave this to me before she passed on, bless her soul. Means ever so much, Tom. Ever so much."

"And . . . we still . . . have a deal?" Tom asked as we walked back though the darkening forest.

"A deal's a deal," he said, crunching across the dry leaves with his heavy shoes. "Don't you worry about that!"

He kept his promise to Tom.

And he bought Sandy a costume key chain that would've fooled a jeweler.

But as it turned out, Tom said he had no use for the money;

his father, he said, would just take it and drink it up. So Dr. Moledinky asked us what he ought to do, and we told him to buy Tom a dog. Which he did: He bought Tom a pedigreed Saint Bernard pup; and one fine day he drove up Drift Road with the top down on his bubble-green 1947 Buick Dina-Flo sedan.

Pauly and I were in my yard when we saw him go past the red-brick Lutheran church. "He's got Tom's dog," Pauly shouted. So we chased after Dr. Moledinky, and by the time we got to Tom's, he already had his arms around a big, fluffy bundle of brown-and-white Saint Bernard.

Dr. Moledinky was smiling like a true benefactor.

"A reward richly deserved, Tom." And bowing to us all, he spun on his heel, got into his car, and drove back down Drift Road.

"I don't know what to say," Tom said thickly.

The pup whimpered and licked Tom's face.

He hugged the pup, and the pup hugged him back.

And from that day forward Tom's cottage never smelled like a wet dog's rug again; it smelled like a Saint Bernard.

My Dad's Fiddle, My Brother's Banjo

When my dad is happy, our house shivers and rings with laughter. But when he's sad, our house is just like he is, quiet. Well, that is, until my dad takes his fiddle out of its rosewood case and rubs rosin on its strings. Then, fiddle in hand, he goes out onto the back porch and makes music.

Usually he plays the mournful melodies of Asia Minor and the Gypsy tunes of ancient Hungary. His people come from Budapest, and he has some of the Gypsy wanderer in him, just like the rest of his family.

Now, my brother Sam is a lot like my dad. But mostly because he inherited his musical talent. If my dad goes out on the porch with his fiddle, you can bet it's not long before Sam comes out and joins him with his banjo.

The banjo's a happy sound—generally. At least that's what people think. But I believe it's just as melancholy as the fiddle, maybe more so. My brother Sam plays it that way, anyhow.

When it rains, soft but not hard, and my dad and my brother are playing together on the back porch, you'd swear there were Gypsies camping in the woods. . . . You can almost hear the impatient hoof-stamp of piebald horses and the kettles of stew being stirred on the fires.

I'm not what you'd call gifted in the music department. Never was, never will be, I don't suppose. But whenever my dad and my brother play, it seems Pauly and I are out roaming the backwoods, listening to them from afar, and I feel as if the music were coming out of me too.

You can hear them for miles, and their melodies are like twine stretched between the trees, which we follow all the way home when it's dark. We go out exploring Mrs. Henshaw's woods, which surround Pauly's house and mine, and phantom strings of blue notes lead us through the night forest, bringing us safely home.

Once, when we are out wandering around Mrs. Henshaw's on a summer evening with the hint of rain in the air and the mushrooms growing in silent hollows, Pauly and I go farther off in the woods than we've ever gone before.

A mile off, in the thickest oak wood ever, we stop in the settling dusk. We can still hear the faint ring of the banjo, the cry of the fiddle.

Yes, they are still playing on the porch.

Then we discover something wonderful.

A great tree, one hundred yards from top to bottom, has toppled in a storm. The roots of this grand old grandfather oak are bearded with wisps of dry grass, and they stretch out like withered fingers, all bony and begging for a drink that never comes to them.

Pauly and I climb into the fallen, upper limbs of the great dead oak. The leaves are dry, crisp. They prattle in the breeze as we walk along the rough-wrinkly trunk.

Once on the tree, the papery forest of branches hides us from the fading light of day. In there it is already night. The scent of dry oak is like the smell of a wine-bottle cork.

We search along and find a place where the leaves have made a small room, a secret fort where we sit and watch the last light leave the sky through an opening in the wall, which is just like a window.

Silent, we sit, thinking our private thoughts.

Quietly listening to the stirring of small night animals that creep out of the ground and rustle the leaves and stretch their wings in the branches above.

Far off, we hear the Gypsy fiddle and the clinging, ringing notes of my brother's banjo.

"When those two are playing," Pauly says, "I almost feel like I want to cry. I don't know who I could say that to but you, Andy."

I want to say something, but there are no words for it, so I say nothing. But just the same, I am wondering at the immensity of it all—the world so large, and our place in it so small.

I mean, here we are, tucked up like a couple of squirrels, and there, way out in the world, are those invisible notes, calling us home.

Doesn't it make you wonder about how magnificent it is?

I realize, then, that I love Pauly as much as my own brother.

And at that moment, especially, I feel it through and through, deep into my bones.

After a little while I whisper to Pauly, "You believe in God?"

"Andy," he says right away, "I believe—"

But before he finishes whatever it is he's going to say, a moth with two moons like owl's eyes painted on its wings floats into our leaf house and lights on Pauly's left arm.

Neither one of us says a word.

What's there to say at a moment like that?

The moth opens and closes its wings—two times, and very slowly. Then it rises into the dusky darkness and disappears out of the open window of the great fallen oak.

At last Pauly answers my question.

"I believe in . . ."

He pauses, wrinkling his nose.

"Whatever that is, that moth, that's what I believe," he says simply.

And I know exactly what he means. Those two moons on the moth's wings that look like owl's eyes, I believe in them. And I believe in the banjo and fiddle tunes that are tied to my blood; and I believe in the failing light and the falling night and the secret sounds of tiny animals moving about; and Pauly himself, and me myself.

Thinking this, as the darkness surrounds us in our fort of leaves, I feel a little shiver go bubbling up my spine.

Time to go.

Time to run like the wind, which suddenly lifts up the dead brown oak leaves and makes them speak crisply in our ear and say to us, *Go home, go home.*

There comes on the rising of the wind the tinkery banjo

and the gay, light-footed fiddle dancing on the air. The banjo is brightening up the pale sickle of a moon, and the fiddle is reaching up into the pearly clouds that hang about in the unstarry sky.

But before the wind can rush us again, we both jump—at the same time—out of that secret hideaway, and striking out upon the earth, we follow those singing notes, running with empty feet, all the way home through the untouchable night of Mrs. Henshaw's woods.

Mrs. Henshaw's Rose

The new-mown grass whispered on the great lawns of Dr. Moledinky, whose distant paradise of meadow and pond, whose perfect world of lane and lawn, made everyone in Berkeley Bend envious.

I remember when Pauly came up to me and said: "Don't it just make you green with envy . . . positively green?"

And even if he hadn't been my best friend, which, of course, he was, I would've answered, as I always did: "I wish I was him!"

Except I didn't. Because I couldn't.

Somehow, that morning, with the dew sparkling on the new-minted leaves and Dr. Moledinky's castle standing boldly in the sun, I felt—well, there was no other way to put it—glum. Not that anything was wrong; it wasn't.

But I looked at my best friend, Pauly, and knew that he, better than anyone, would understand. The morning was, somehow, jinxed. I told him as much.

Pauly said, "I know just what you mean."

And then he looked just the way I felt; or the other way around.

"It's hard to put your finger on it," I said. We were sitting on Pauly's front lawn, looking out at the world.

"Everything's there," I confided, "just like it's supposed to be—"

"Just like it always is," Pauly said.

"Yeah," I said. "But something—"

"—somewhere . . ."

"—is missing."

We stared up at Dr. Moledinky's castle, which usually filled us, just like everybody else in Berkeley Bend, with the glad tidings of envy. Well, isn't that what guys like Dr. Moledinky, who are rich as Croesus and as merciless as Midas, are supposed to make you feel?

I don't know, but it seems it's the Moledinkys of the world who run things and who have it all their own way. He could be as rude as he wanted to be, or as kind and courtly—it didn't matter, because people would always forgive or forget his unlikely actions, and credit him for the rest.

As a result, he acted "anywhichway," which was how Pauly put it. "That's old Moledinky," he'd say, excusing anything the man did that was out of the ordinary—which, in fact, was practically everything. If Moledinky walked to O'Connor's Market in his boxers, nobody would say he was underdressed. And if he wore a full tux with a bowler hat to a meeting of the Parents' Association, nobody would say he was overdressed.

I guess guys like Moledinky can get away with anything.

You see, they have all the gold—and it shows.

As for the rest of us, well, it's our tough luck if we don't get any breaks, because, as Dr. Moledinky says often enough: "You want it, go get it."

Pauly and I looked at each other and we both thought the same thing; it came to us at precisely the same moment.

There we were in front of Pauly's house, looking up at Dr. Moledinky's castle. The dove-gray stonework, the ivy walls, the stained-glass windows . . . and there, right opposite Dr. Moledinky's driveway, was the half-built, lopsided, crooked shack of poor old Mrs. Henshaw.

"That's the saddest sight I ever saw," Pauly said remorsefully.

"Yeah," I agreed. "It's what's wrong with the morning, isn't it? Funny how we never noticed it before. . . ."

There was Dr. Moledinky's great emerald lawn, and just below it, the rust wooded hill of Mrs. Henshaw. His yard was teeming with flowers; hers was overrun with rosehip brambles. And where he had ivy decorating his walls, she had thorns thicker than ten-penny nails.

"Poor old Mrs. Henshaw," Pauly said again, shaking his head.

"Don't say anything more," I said. "She could hear us whispering about her right now." Which was why we didn't talk about her that much. You see, there were a lot of curious rumors about Mrs. Henshaw and her tar-paper shack.

Some said she was a witch.

Some said she wasn't.

The trouble was, we didn't feel sorry for her. That is, the

town didn't. Not really. Because people were always saying, "She made her bed, let her lie in it."

I never really knew what that meant. I don't think anyone did; it just sounded good. Like any excuse.

"You know," I said to Pauly, "I wonder if we could get close enough to Mrs. Henshaw's house to see into those dark windows?"

"Who'd want to?" he said, peeling the bark off a willow stick.

"Well, I'd kind of like to see inside," I said.

Pauly looked surprised. Then, nodding, he said: "I always wanted to—when I was a little kid. But not anymore." He peeled the willow wand with his thumb and the bark came off clean, showing the white milky wood.

"All right." He sighed. "When do you want to look inside?"

"Tomorrow night."

He flicked the air with his wand, making a singing sound.

"I'll be there."

The following night we were crawling along on our bellies through the bramble bushes, trying to get close to that tarpaper shack. And it was like crawling across eternity to get there. There were excavations here and there just like foxholes, bombed out or dug out, places you had to crawl down into and out of before you could get going again.

Pauly got discouraged first. "By the time we arrive at her doorstep," he said thickly, "we're each going to be wearing a beard!"

"Mrs. Henshaw doesn't have a doorstep," I remarked, cranking along on my elbows like the comic book GI, Sgt. Rock, under fire. All around my head—and Pauly's—were the barbed-wire sticker bushes.

"Good thing we got the moon," Pauly said idly when we finally lay back and took a rest.

I glanced at the spiraling wire, green as dragon's blood, and the moon hanging high overhead like a big silver street-lamp.

We were lying on our backs, breathing easy and talking in whispers when, halfway across the barbed green no-man's land, the door of the shack swung wide.

We froze. Like a couple of rabbits.

Out into the moon-washed night Mrs. Henshaw sailed like the witch she was rumored to be, out, out, light as a legend, and then, *kerthump*. If Dr. Moledinky himself had hopped past on a one-legged horse, we couldn't have been more surprised.

"Who took my porch?" came a wobbly voice.

"What porch?" Pauly whispered.

"Shhh," I hissed. I covered my head with my hands.

There we were, pinned down in the bramble bushes, and Mrs. Henshaw was struggling to get to her feet. If she saw us, we were dead! And what if she really was a witch? . . .

"Where's my porch?" she demanded of the moon.

And the moon, saying nothing, made white roses of the brambles, while we scrunched down in the shadows.

"What do we do now?" Pauly said. I could see the silver beads of sweat brightening his brow.

"How the hell should I know?" I said through my teeth.

"So we just stay here all night, while that old witch—"

At the mention of that word, a dry, thin, moon-pale voice said: "Who's there?"

In the surrounding silence, an owl swam over our heads.

The voice moaned moonily, "Hiding—are we?"

From the prison of the brambles, we watched Mrs. Henshaw climb to her knees and, using a piece of old scaffolding for a crutch, haul herself up. Then she began to drag her body toward our hiding place.

As she came on, we heard her mumble: "Well, I'll . . ."

The voice was dust.

We lay low, our hearts thumping, and the thorn coils held us in their grip.

"She can't see us," Pauly mouthed silently.

The heavy foot, the thump of the makeshift cane, the dragged weight drew nearer.

"What say?" Mrs. Henshaw barked at the moon. Her head was cocked to one side as the white light fell on the folds of her baggy housedress. She took another step.

I lay flat as a coin. Pauly's nose, knee-level to a snake, breathed on me.

Mrs. Henshaw came grawking into the secrecy of the thorns, crunching them underfoot. A distant dog howled.

Maybe the suspense was too much. I don't know. Anyway, suddenly Pauly bolted. He jumped up, curtained with rosehips. Tripping over me, he bashed his way into the open air.

Mrs. Henshaw swung like a moonlit cyclone, grabbed

Pauly by the collar. She was big, all right. And even leaning on that staff, she was able to seize Pauly and hold him fast.

"You better come out, too," she snorted, glancing in my direction.

Immediately I heaved myself up and began wriggling free of the rosehip harness that had fixed itself to my clothes.

"We didn't do anything," Pauly protested. His T-shirt was torn, and he had the dust-dark face of a chimney sweep.

"What do you have to say for yourselves," Mrs. Henshaw rasped, "stealing porches and hiding out in a poor old woman's garden?"

"Garden?" Pauly squeaked.

Mrs. Henshaw.

There she was, at last: a great mountain of a woman with the moon perched on her shoulder like a silver bird. She seemed, throwing her shadow over us, to have grown out of the ground.

I glanced down.

And found myself staring at Mrs. Henshaw's bare feet. They were white, wondrously white, and huge.

I couldn't help myself. I really couldn't. The moment I saw those great big moon-white feet, I started laughing.

Mrs. Henshaw put Pauly down. And turned her full attention to me. "What's so funny?" she said. Her voice had an edge like a knife.

I stopped laughing, shrugged. "I dunno."

It was so strange—I just wasn't afraid of her. Not even a little bit. I don't know why; I don't know that I ever will.

But she could feel the strangeness.

Mrs. Henshaw leaned closer to me, and the moon slipped off her shoulder, and her face was right next to mine, and I still wasn't afraid of her, and she could sense it too.

"Oh my!" she sighed. She let go of Pauly and sat down with a groan.

"What's wrong?" Pauly asked, rubbing his arm where she'd grabbed him.

Mrs. Henshaw sat in the dirt, sobbing. Her shoulders shook and the tears silvered her face, and she didn't bother to wipe them away. She continued crying as if we weren't there.

"I'll help you," I said weakly. I meant it, but I didn't know what else to say. I'd never seen anyone cry like that before. The tears, her shoulders, the way she sat down, the sound her voice made when she cried, like a kid . . . well, not exactly. That was the weird part. Mrs. Henshaw, crying like that, didn't sound like a kid or an old woman, either. She sounded more like a . . . young lady, a young, pretty lady.

Then, as suddenly as it started, it stopped.

"Do you know my name?" she asked, wiping the tears away from her eyes.

"Everyone in Berkeley Bend knows that," I told her.

She took a deep breath and got to her feet, with Pauly and me helping, and then we were walking very slowly toward the tar-paper shack, her bare feet making little puffs of dust in the ancient excavated dirt where her lawn should've been.

"Fell off my porch, and I don't even have one. Isn't that the dumbest thing you ever heard?" she lamented as she limped along.

We walked her to the door of her house. She stood for a while, breathing. Then, without looking back, she hoisted herself up and asked us to come in.

Pauly and I flashed looks of amazement, which we covered quickly. Then we stepped up over the threshold and into the house we'd wanted to have a look at for so long.

The interior of Mrs. Henshaw's shack was bare; as unfinished inside as outside. The floors were only partly put up—holes showed through to the cellar, which was all dark earth. And the walls, if you could call them such, were sheets of rain-warped plywood, all peeling apart.

It was not a house, not even a shack house—it was a skeleton of a dwelling, a paper plan held together with splinters and tacks, knots and nails. One electric bulb dangled from a frayed black cord, and when she clicked it on, banishing the moonbeams, the shadows crept about like moving animals.

"Cocoa?" she asked pleasantly.

Pauly and I said, "Sure."

And while she busied herself over a Coleman stove, pumping it up, we continued to look around, our mouths open. How long had she been here? Well, we didn't really know, but it was a long, long time.

What emptiness greeted our eyes. What quarters for rats, bats, moths, and mice—though we saw none. There was no furniture anywhere—not a cinder block to sit on, not an orange crate nor a soda box. There was nothing there, nothing at all. Except, of course, Mrs. Henshaw, the little camp stove, and a few cups and plates lying on a newspaper.

We squatted, as she did, to be polite. And sipped our hot cocoa, as she did, when she did—because, frankly, neither of us knew what, if anything, we should, or could, say. So we sat and sipped. And every once and a while darted an eye here or there, to see if we'd missed anything. No, we hadn't.

Then Pauly did a funny thing. He said, "Mrs. Henshaw, can I ask you something?" And he asked it like he'd known her all of his life, which, in some sense, I suppose he really had.

She turned her great head in his direction and, looking him up and down, nodded silently. I noticed that though she was very large, her features were somehow quite delicate; as if belonging to a much smaller person. Her eyes were greenish brown, veiled. You couldn't look at her very long, or she'd glance away.

"You can ask me anything you want," she replied honestly to Pauly. And from the way she said it, I imagined that she also believed she'd known Pauly her whole life, which, of course, she hadn't.

He said, then, two words.

Two small, empty-sounding words that were bigger, far bigger than Mrs. Henshaw's house. In fact, they were the largest words anybody's ever spoken, anywhere, on earth.

"What happened?" he asked.

It made my heart stop. I gulped some hot chocolate, even though there wasn't any left, and pretended to swallow.

Mrs. Henshaw came over to Pauly, and she said so softly

that we could barely hear her: "Nobody's asked me that for such a long, long time. . . ."

Her brown-green eyes swept the room. She inhaled deeply. I saw that, once, long ago, she had been, if not beautiful, handsome. Her hair, steely gray, was probably once blond; her eyebrows were the color of fawnskin.

"Such a long time," she said. Her voice was mist.

Then she reached into the front of her faded housedress and drew out a gold locket on a chain. She placed her thumb on the edge of it, clicked it open.

We saw, for a brief second, the face of a man we'd never known. A soldier, uniformed, smiling.

Husband? Friend? Lover?

"Dead," she said. Then snapped it shut, tucked it back.

Pauly and I were wondering what to say, when she said it for us: "Look around," she remarked, almost joyfully. "All this was his work!"

Our eyes flew from beam to header and from rafter to joist, and back again to the clean-swept, well-worn floor that had never seen a drop of varnish, oil, or wax.

"Well?" she asked pleasantly, "what do you think of his work?"

I had no idea what to say, but Pauly answered, "Beautiful."

"You think I'm insane, don't you?" The voice was suddenly cold.

She hooked us with her eyes and gave a hollow laugh.

"Oh, my!" she exclaimed. She walked around the floor, and it creaked against her weight. "The whole town thinks I'm crazy, doesn't it?"

This time I answered before Pauly. "Who cares what they think?" I said.

"Yes," she answered in that cotton soft voice, "who indeed?"

We moved toward the door and hastened outside into the white night. It felt good to be breathing fresh air again, away from the shabby wooden building, the tacked-together house that had never had a chance to be a home.

Outside then, hopping onto the hills of briars, the rosehips strung like barbed wire across a beachhead, we heard Mrs. Henshaw say something to us.

"He died out there," she said, "during the war."

And for the first time, Pauly and I knew the true meaning of no-man's land.

"Well, you can go. No one's holding you prisoner. Go on, get!" She flung her right hand at us while covering her eyes with her left.

"He likes you," she said, pointing to me.

And then I was running after Pauly, running like the wind that rides a horse's mane, running like the rivers of tears that were streaming down Mrs. Henshaw's face.

I never spoke to Mrs. Henshaw again after that.

Neither, so far as I know, did Pauly.

But we never made fun of her, either. We used to watch her trying to make some flowers grow in front of her bombed-out yard with the brambles and foxholes. But we never said anything to her. The flowers turned brown, shriveled, and disappeared. Then, about a month after that moonlit night, Mrs. Henshaw died of a heart attack. We read her obituary in the

Courier Dispatch and it said that she was survived by no one, and that the town was taking possession of her property. It also said that there had been a Mr. Henshaw, who was killed in World War I.

Gassed, the newspaper said.

In a foxhole.

I planted a flower for her then, a red, red rose.

And it grew in and out of the dirt piles and sprouted flames that licked about the briars, and always reminded me of blood spots on a stiff new green uniform.

Doctor Moledinky's Animal Museum

There is a big lodge at the top of a tree-shaded hill, and that's where Dr. Moledinky's headquarters are. You walk through the main door and into a private sanctuary of bottled, bagged, mottled, dead, stuffed, and stored animals.

It's open to the public, nine to four, weekdays and weekends.

My mom drives me up there at the beginning of the summer to see if Dr. Moledinky will hire me for the job of animal attendant. Every summer he hires a few kids to help out, and Pauly's already got a job, so I want one too.

We wander around, my mom and I, moving through the interior of the museum. We've got an appointment; Dr. Moledinky's waiting to see us.

We step among tables decked out with all kinds of curious creatures; all of them dead.

I wonder, why do live people like to look at dead animals?

I don't myself, but other people must like it; otherwise why would there be a place like this?

There is a bottle full of golden fluid. Inside, forever afloat, is a two-headed king snake with blue eyes, robin's-egg blue; and dead, very dead.

Then there is a stuffed possum with its right front paw raised in the air as if it's asking a question or searching for something. The possum's tongue looks like glazed clay. I touch it, real quick—cold and clammy feeling! The beady little eyes are glass, and it stares out of a head full of stuffing, dead.

My mom is speaking softly to me as we walk up the aisle to Dr. Moledinky's office.

"Making a dead animal look alive is called *taxidermy,*" she tells me.

"It's *stupidermy,* you ask me."

She smiles. I know that she hates seeing this as much as I do. She loves animals—that're alive.

I'm not so sure that I want to work here now. What is there to learn about a possum that will never again wrap its tail around a hickory limb?

What good's a two-headed king snake, dead and doubled up in a bottle?

The one-headed, alive kind are able to slip through your hand like water, and that feels good to the touch.

Besides, I don't like the smell of the museum: all must and dust and crust. I touch the head of an ancient dried-up skunk mounted on a board, and its fur has a thick coat of the dandruff of the dead.

In the back of the museum there is a door that leads to a

small office. There Dr. Moledinky is holed up, buried in piles of paper, ledgers, account books. We can see him as we proceed toward his office—like a badger digging away in his burrow.

We enter and he looks up immediately. He's a small man, broad of shoulder, with a big barrel chest and a square face. He looks just like Teddy Roosevelt on safari. And he is dressed the part too, with his bush jacket and his round-rimmed eyeglasses and even a green felt hat with the brim folded up on one side.

As we walk into his office, he says, "Don't mind the mess, I'll be with you in a minute."

His voice is sort of gravelly, and low. There are a couple of folding chairs and we seat ourselves in them.

I can almost hear my mom say "lower element" under her breath. But not really, for Dr. Moledinky's actually been written up in her favorite magazine, *Reader's Digest.* He can't be low, anyway—he's too rich.

We sit down, and Dr. Moledinky closes the book he is consulting.

"Come for the job, have we?" he asks.

My mom smiles. "My son Andy loves animals."

I nod in agreement, and try not to think about the piles of dead ones outside the office.

"Can you lift an eighty-pound feeding tray?" he questions.

"I lift weights."

"And your work experience is . . . ?"

"I do lots of things."

"And they are?"

His round-rimmed glasses gleam under the overhead light. His eyes are very large and intent and scrutinous, and they bore into me.

"Well, let's see . . ."

I try to think of all the household jobs I've had, but my eye kind of catches on some deer hooves on the knotty-pine wall behind Dr. Moledinky's head. The hooves are holding something up—a thing that I can't figure out what it is. . . . It looks like a shriveled walking stick, very shiny and bright, as if shellacked.

I wonder, could it be a baby elephant's trunk?

Dr. Moledinky follows my gaze, and grins.

"If you don't mind"—he chuckles—"taking your eyes off my bull's-penis cane, we can come back to earth and talk about your application for a job."

Now I hear my mom whispering under her breath, for real.

Dr. Moledinky's done it—automatically lowered himself into the lower element—with that cane.

So I rattle on about my various jobs: "I've worked at Hilltop Florist as a delivery boy; I've also delivered papers for the *Courier Dispatch*; I've shoveled snowy driveways and sold greeting cards for a card company in Minneapolis; now I'm mowing lawns all over Berkeley Bend."

I feel Dr. Moledinky's safari-seeing eyes probe into my face, seeking my true identity. Am I friend or foe, he is wondering, predator or prey?

"And what makes you think you could feed my animals?" he asks.

"I like animals."

"You may hate them before you're through—"

"Don't you think that is a bit harsh?" my mom says.

I can feel her stiffen at my side. There is nothing in this world that my mom appreciates more than animals.

I'm sitting there now, wondering how a whole town can admire this man so much. And I'm also wondering how he acquired so much wealth and high standing. Aside from his looks, which are commanding, I think he's awfully (I have to agree with my mom) lower element.

But who cares? The main thing is that I want the job—anything to be near the live animals outside. I hope I never have to dust off any of the pelts or polish the bottles in the dead part of the museum, and I hope he hires me as a feeder because that's really what I want to do, and that's why I came.

"Fifty cents an hour," he says sharply, pressing his fingertips together. I watch as he extends them. His fingers look like a spider doing push-ups on a mirror.

"I am still uncertain as to whether you can really lift a hundred-pound tray of animal food."

"You said it was eighty pounds before," my mom says.

"You were listening." He sighs. "Now then—can you?"

"I guess so."

"How much do you weigh?"

I tell him that I weigh about eighty-six pounds.

He frowns deeply, clears his throat.

"Can you raise that moose head off the floor over there?" he wants to know.

"I guess so."

"Then do so."

I get up and walk across the room, where there's a great big musty old moose head that looks like it's been there since before the Civil War, and I bend down and try to give it a pull. The moose head doesn't budge.

"Try again, lad; put your back into it."

I do. But the head must weigh a ton. I can't raise it an inch. I shake my head in defeat and sit down next to my mom, who is smiling triumphantly.

"Well," she says in a cheerful voice, "does that mean he doesn't get the job?"

Dr. Moledinky smacks his lips and bursts out laughing.

"That's okay," I say. "I don't need the job anyway."

"You've got the job, lad, don't worry."

"Think so?"

"Know so—I own the joint. If I say you're hired, hired you be!"

Meekly I ask, "But what about the moose head—I couldn't move it a millimeter."

"Neither can I," Dr. Moledinky roared, "neither can I. Thing weighs a ton. Taxidermist must've filled it with cement—there's no wall in the place strong enough to hold it up."

He smacks his lips again and looks me over from head to toe.

"You'll do, and if not, I'll just have you mounted like the rest of them. Is that all right with you, son?"

"As long as you don't put me in that bottle with the two-headed king snake."

Dr. Moledinky lets out a bull's roar again.

"The boy's got a sense of humor," he says. "I like that."

"I get it from my dad."

"I like that too," he says, raising his bristly upper lip and showing his fine set of straight white teeth.

"Can I ask what are you writing?" I say.

"I don't know—can you?"

I know the trick, and correct myself quickly.

"I mean, *may* I ask?"

"Sure may." He chuckles.

"Yes," my mom adds curiously, "I'd like to know as well."

"You both shall know." He beams. "I am engaged in writing what will be a great book."

I think, looking at him now, he is more Teddy than Moledinky. The spitting image of the man who headed up San Juan Hill.

I admire his thick wrists, the cords of muscle on them. And his neck, like a post. And his perfect teeth.

"Yes, a great, a very great book—the summation of my life's work, my final achievement."

"Are you being modest?" my mom questions with a small smile.

"Don't believe in it," he snaps. "Modesty's for fools, and those who can't get ahead in the world. For those of us who know where we stand, why—"

"Indeed," my mom replies.

"So what's the book going to be called?" I put in. I certainly don't want my mom getting into a scrape with my new boss, not just yet anyway.

He brightens up like a high beam whenever you mention his book, his achievement.

"The working title's *Doctor Moledinky's Answer—To Everything.*"

He pauses to allow the flavor of this to soak in.

My mom is looking at her lap.

"Catchy title, don't you think?" Dr. Moledinky asks. He rubs his chin and it makes a scratchy sound.

"It certainly doesn't commit the sin of modesty," my mom sighs, and she gets up to leave.

Dr. Moledinky thumps me on the back.

"How's about we go meet the animals?"

We walk out, the three of us, out of the musty museum into the sunny daylight, where I meet my friends Ally, Wally, Buzz, Sandy, and Cindy for the very first time.

Doctor Moledinky's Castle

One day, near the end of summer, Pauly and I were catching ribbon snakes that lived in the roots of his willow tree. There must have been a migration of them. They kept pouring out of the cracks between the roots. We were waiting and some of them sluiced right through our fingers, but plenty of others came out of the ground and fell into our hands and didn't want to leave, for as everyone knows, snakes like human contact because they're cold-blooded and humans are warm-blooded; although sometimes I think it ought to go the other way around.

"You know," Pauly said, "I bet we could sell some of these to Dr. Moledinky." He had about a half dozen little black-and-yellow, lightning-tongued ribbons flowing out of his shirt pocket and spilling on the ground.

"I doubt he'd buy anything so common," I said.

"Maybe they're an everyday kind of snake, but look at how many of 'em we got here!"

He was right about that; there was a small river of striped snakes at our feet.

In the cool shade of Pauly's weeping willow, with its ever-raining curtain of waterfall green all around us, we had a perfect hideout. A place to talk and make secret plans. When we were inside the gold-green, sun-flecked willow hideout, we seemed to come up with great and wonderful ideas.

This day being no exception, Pauly lay back and, putting his hands behind his head, looked into the winking and blinking wind-blown leaves of the willow tree. The ribbon snakes resumed their magical migration, using Pauly's face as a highway to heaven. Out of the roots and onto Pauly's arm, over his shoulder and onto the trunk of the willow tree. From there, upward—who knows where, or why. . . .

"It feels funny when they tickle your nose with their tongue," Pauly commented.

"Yeah."

"It feels really weird when they go through your hair."

"Yeah."

I wasn't listening; I was thinking. For some reason, I suddenly got it into my head to find out what it was that lived inside Dr. Moledinky's moat. It was driving me crazy, thinking about it. Dr. Moledinky had a castle and a moat. He also had an animal museum and a mint-green 1947 Buick Dina-Flo sedan.

But the best thing that he owned, by far, was that moat. The castle sat on a hill above the town of Berkeley Bend. Below the gray turrets and somber walls was an emerald lawn that took three lawn boys a week and a half to mow. At the bottom of the lawn, where it nearly met Mountain Avenue, there was a black moat of devilish slime with lily pads, water weeds, cattails—but there were no frogs or fish of any kind. The moat moved sluggishly along like sludge. On either side of it were skunk cabbages, great fat leafy things that smelled terrible.

"What are you thinking about?" Pauly said. His red-haired head was laced with snake tails.

"I'm wondering about Dr. Moledinky's moat."

"What about it?"

"Well, I'm wondering," I explained, "what might be living in it. You know, what kind of creature."

"We've been through that before," said Pauly, plucking a particularly lengthy black ribbon out of his reddish locks and holding it by the tail.

"Remember when your dog ran away and we found its bones by Dr. Moledinky's moat?"

Pauly released the snake, and it made a slender exit into the grass. He frowned. "Never could prove anything," he said sorely.

"Mainly," I announced, "because Dr. Moledinky's such a big shot in Berkeley Bend. No one wants to imagine that he's got a live alligator or something swimming around in his moat. But if we were to—"

"—find one," Pauly clicked.

"—some night. . . ." I completed.

Pauly's face lit up. "How 'bout tonight?" he added. His eyes fizzed with impishness. "Just like the time we bivouacked old Mrs. Henshaw's house and—"

"Only different," I interrupted, "because this time we won't get caught, will we?" I put in that last to remind him that not getting caught means not making noise, and not making noise means shutting up, and shutting up is the best procedure in any case.

That night I slipped out the attic window, crawled down the drainpipe. I stuck my hands in my pockets to see if I had everything we needed: flashlight, nylon cord, small lead pipe. Pauly, who was waiting on the ground when I dropped down, showed me what he'd brought—flashlight, length of chain, and his pump-action air rifle. "That's only in case things get out of hand," he told me. I showed him my stuff. "What's the lead pipe for?" he asked.

"Well, did you ever see *Ramar of the Jungle* on the late matinee?"

I knew that he had, because we usually watched it together on the old Zenith up in my attic bedroom. As I've mentioned once before, that television set, like most of the stored-away stuff in the attic, was all but useless. It was as big as an oven and it burned as hot as one too—especially when the sun was beating on the roof and making the boards on the ceiling drip pine sap on our heads. That's why we liked to watch *Ramar* up there; it was steamy and full of atmosphere.

One time Pauly asked me, "How come your parents don't fix this place up better?"

"They think I like to live like a squirrel," I told him, which was the truth—I did. However, the other reason was that they were usually too busy with their own affairs to worry about mine. I think they trusted that if I wanted my bedroom to look neater, I'd say something about it. As it happened, though, I liked it just the way it was—as an attic. Only, sometimes, when the roof cooled off on a summer night, it made the creepiest noises: all kinds of clickings and creakings. Then I wished—but only then—that I had a more conventional place to sleep.

"So, what's the lead pipe for?" Pauly asked again.

"Don't you remember when Ramar was being chased by a crocodile and he pulled out his knife and shoved it in the croc's mouth, pinning its jaws open?"

Pauly screwed up his face, said: "C-o-o-l, I remember now."

We proceeded on through the night, going into Mrs. Henshaw's woods to Dr. Moledinky's castle. Her old ramshackle, unfinished house looked even more empty and desolate now that she was gone. Pauly said: "There lived the poorest woman in Berkeley Bend."

I said, "I don't think she was so poor, Pauly."

He stepped on a stick, which made a loud cracking noise.

"Break your back, if you do that again," I warned, and said again, "I don't think she was poor."

"She had an empty old house full of cobwebs."

I told him: "She had lots of memories."

Pauly made a snuffing noise with his nose. "I wonder why she never married again? Imagine if she'd gotten hitched to Dr. Moledinky. . . . Then she'd have been really rich."

We were coming out of the woods and into an open field.

The green, gloss bottomlands of the great Moledinky estate were visible through the night-breathing trees. There was the moat, glittering tunefully in the dark. The castle on the rise above cast a shadow cold as black iron.

"Pauly," I chuckled as we came out of the brush, "you say the darnedest things. I know for a fact that Mrs. Henshaw wouldn't've paid any notice to old Dr. Moledinky, even if he had been madly in love with her. She was so in love with her husband. Don't you remember?"

"Yeah," Pauly said, suddenly disinterested. "Hey, will you get a load of that moat!" He reeled backward as if staggered by the sight, but I knew that he was only playacting.

Presently there was a disturbance on the surface of the water. Away off in the blue, soft hills, a horse whinnied crazily. Then a dog howled thinly on the wind, and the thing in the moat, whatever it was, curved backward and forward, bank to bank; and the water swirled and came to life as a finny shape appeared and descended into the depths.

Pauly and I gave an involuntary shudder. The black moat of Dr. Moledinky revealed a shape that was long and sinuous. The thing that was in there was slicker than oil and quiet as a mole and more wicked than sliding down a banister made of razor blades.

"What was that?" Pauly asked. His mouth was open and his face was white as a grub worm. I watched him settle the butt of his pump gun against the inside heel on his paratrooper boot, and then he began pumping it up. The more times he pumped, the harder the force on the pellet lodged in the chamber when he pulled the trigger.

"You gonna shoot an elephant with that thing?" I questioned.

Pauly didn't look at me, but he kept pumping, and puffing for breath. Finally he lay in the grass. "I got a better idea." He sighed. "Let's go back to my place and get my dad's double-barreled shotgun."

I glanced at the moat. The starlight's glimmer was like the skin of an iridescent animal. Then the water spanked the banks, and something ugly heaved itself out of the moat and began to crawl in our direction.

Pauly leaped to his feet with the spring of an alley cat. Without looking where he was shooting, he fired into the damp grass. I heard the lead pellet go *thunk* into the earth, but the thing came on, lumbering in our direction.

I buried my hand in my pocket, took out my flashlight, and flicked it on. A misty oval of bluey light fell on the strangest creature I have ever seen in my life.

"Don't shoot," I warned Pauly. "I think it's some kind of miniature dinosaur."

Nonetheless, Pauly, pumping his gun, squeezed off another shot. The pellet went *whunk* over the creature's head into the embankment of the moat.

"Another random shot like that and I'll be forced to fire one of my own," a pencil-thin voice said.

Astonished, we looked all around. I drove my beam around the moat and the surrounding grounds, but there was nothing there. The night was warm, and the moat gave off the ripe, cruddy smell of standing water. As we glanced about, both of us training our beams in all directions so that the night was pierced by swords of light, we heard a groan. Immediately our flashlights—as if they had minds of their own—swung down onto the grass.

"My god, it's some kind of walking catfish," Pauly wailed.

"That is precisely what it is," Dr. Moledinky said curtly, stepping from behind a magnolia bush.

"Dr. Moledinky!" Pauly gasped.

"Who else would own a prize Boca Raton walking—some say stalking—catfish, I would like to know?" Dr. Moledinky asked, his voice as cold as the moat over which he and the catfish presided.

"Gee willickers," Pauly shouted, "look at all those spines around its head."

"Be careful you don't step on one," Dr. Moledinky said in an acid tone. "Or you won't be around to say 'gee willickers' anymore."

He was wearing a multipocketed safari shirt and a flat-brimmed felt hat with a leopard-skin hat band. He had on shorts and high rubber boots, and there was a net in his hand and a holster on his belt.

"Come to daddy, thornycums," he said teasingly. Then Dr. Moledinky dipped the large net over the slippery, slimy, slowly slithery, half-legged, half-gilled toad-faced catfish creature from Boca Raton. In the net the thing's head lolled heavily, and the poisonous spikes growing out of its skull gleamed against the foul moat breath rising off the sickly-looking water. We watched as he carried the net over to the black, bubbly surface and dropped the creature into the water with a loud liquid *plop!*

"Well, gentlemen," Dr. Moledinky said, "is that a wrap?"

"A what?" Pauly said. He was standing there gripping his gun like a trooper.

"Shall we call it a night, then?" Dr. Moledinky remarked, stroking his jaw.

We waited, said nothing.

Then, "What's it going to take to chase you little trespassers home?" Dr. Moledinky questioned again.

Nearby, a mockingbird sang one sleepy note from a mulberry bush. Dr. Moledinky squooshed his toes inside his rubber boots.

"So what will it take?" he said again into the steamy moat-drooling night.

And this time Pauly spoke up: "How about a tour of your castle?" He looked at Dr. Moledinky admiringly.

"Is that—all?" Dr. Moledinky said, his tongue lingering playfully on the word *all.* Then he clicked his tongue against his palette, *tsk, tsk,* and said, "Come along then."

And he strode off into the flashlit field, following the course of the moat, and, fascinated, we followed him across the vast lawn at which we'd gazed from afar, dreaming of the day—or night—that we might see the inside of Dr. Moledinky's castle.

And then we were crossing the magnificent moat, walking over a real wooden drawbridge, our footsteps echoing below on the still water. Soon we would enter the secret chambers of the richest man alive.

Pauly whispered, "Can you believe this? He's taking us into the castle—and all we had to do was ask!"

We went swishing through the swampy night, sensing unknown presences that filled the darkness all around us. Dr. Moledinky's glossy rubber boots squashed two steps ahead. And then—we were there, stepping under the low stone arch of a wooden door made for a gnome. As the door creaked on its cast-iron hinges, I took one last glance at the soaring stone exterior of the building that went straight into the fog sky and touched the milky stars with the spires of its owl-eared turrets, ducked through the inky vault, and breathed in the richly enchanting odor of castle.

Inside, it was dark. The darkest dark ever an eye beheld.

"Stay here, boys," Dr. Moledinky commanded. "I'm going to see about a light."

"What's he mean by that?" Pauly said softly.

"I dunno."

Pauly leaned close, cupping his hand over his mouth. I could barely see him in the dark. In a moment Dr. Moledinky reappeared in a brilliant cone of white-gold light, swinging a Coleman lantern in his right hand. The shadows around him thickened and thinned as the lantern revolved, flooding the huge room with its burning beacon.

"Now then, boys," Dr. Moledinky said. "What is it, exactly, that you came here to see?" But before either Pauly or I could answer, he swung the Coleman. The golden mantle was so intense, it blinded us, as well as made the hollows of Dr. Moledinky's face appear monstrous and large. He was all nose one minute, all mustache the next.

Dr. Moledinky gestured grandly, "my empire under one roof."

We stared, blinking, into the blackness. There was nothing but the shadows that fled before the flaring Coleman; around them lay the great unseeable emptiness that was the castle's interior.

"Are there no . . . lights in here?" Pauly asked.

"Light?" Dr. Moledinky shouted. "Why, son, the absence of light is darkness, don't you agree? And yet it is still the very presence of light itself. For light, young man, is born of its opposite, dark. The Lord said, 'Let there be light!' And lo, verily, there was!"

He swung the Coleman up and down, beckoning the frantic, fluttering bat shapes to come and go; to sweep the room and suck it dry, to lay it bare and soak it with the blackest of ink.

"He's nuttier than old Mrs. Henshaw," Pauly sputtered in my ear.

I was thinking the same thing. It was as if, once surrounded by his castle, Dr. Moledinky had become wackier than ever.

"I am working," Dr. Moledinky said, "on the experiment of a lifetime. In the secrecy of my laboratory, which is the cool grotto of my castle, things are taking shape."

As he said this, I saw some new shadows steal across the floor on tiny tattery, rattery feet.

"You must think it strange for a man to live like this," he said gravely.

Pauly answered, "I don't think it's strange. I just can't see anything in here—so I don't know what it is—"

"—or what it isn't," I finished.

"I see what you mean." Dr. Moledinky grinned. He was resting his chin on his palm; the hissing Coleman dangled from his other hand.

"Maybe we should go now," Pauly suggested meekly.

"Sure," I added, "we've seen enough already, no need—"

"Don't be absurd," Dr. Moledinky said, as if his hospitality had suddenly been offended. He sucked in a deep breath and said, "Why, I've not even shown you the tanks where my baby catfish are incubating, or the freezer room where I store the ones that die, or the—"

"Why do they die?" I asked.

"All things die," he returned. "We die a little with each breath that we take, if you get my meaning. Well, this is silly, gandering like a bunch of geese—come along and I'll show you."

Once again he started off, boots a-squishing, the Coleman gobbling up the darkness as we went along in single file.

Finally my eyes adjusted just enough to perceive the huge cavernous cathedral of a room that we were in. There were no separations, no stairs, no rooms—just the massive empty belly of the castle itself. The floor was made of tile, the walls of stone. There was nothing in there but a bunch of white horizontal freezers and some large green tanks full of water.

Dr. Moledinky held the Coleman so we could see his treasures, the little incubating catfish. From tank spawn to frozen fin, he had the whole life cycle of the fish down pat. And that was that; the castle was nothing more than a breeding ground for a bunch of low-class fish uglier than a hammerhead shark.

I experienced a sinking feeling.

Dr. Moledinky, the billionaire of Berkeley Bend, was falling fast in my sight, falling so low there'd be no more man in another minute. Was the whole thing—even the man himself—a hoax?

Where were the Egyptian scrolls and statues of mystic cats?

Where were the tapestries woven of dreams from the Silk Road of ancient China?

Where were the Burmese tiger rugs and the heads of kudus and the ostrich-wing fans from the smoky dunes of the Sahara?

Where was . . . the missing magic of Dr. Moledinky?

Pauly, whose knack for words never failed, said it himself: "Hey, Dr. Moledinky," he remarked emptily, "what good are all these catfish?"

Dr. Moledinky turned on a dime and set the Coleman on the floor, where it burned a million seething holes in the black curtain that hung about our shoulders. "Lobe-fin fish," he uttered. "What good are lobe-fin catfish?"

Pauly and I shrugged.

Then nodded at the same time.

"Yeah," he said.

"Yeah," I echoed.

Dr. Moledinky gestured with his hands as if he were shaping a vase of wet clay. He pointed to the great tanks lined up around the room and said: "Here, in these quiet tombs—the freezers—and in these silent breeders—the aquariums—we have all that life is." Along the upper region of his brow, his eyebrows arched like woolly bears.

Pauly said, "What's that?"

"Punctualism!" Dr. Moledinky snapped.

"Huh?" said Pauly, completely confused.

Dr. Moledinky faced the enormous theater of blackness beyond the Coleman's glow. He held his hands on his chest, and it appeared that he imagined he was addressing an audience, because he certainly wasn't—at that moment—talking to either of us. "Punc-tu-al-ism," he pronounced; the word went rolling off his lips into the chamber of soft-kept secrets, the unborn empty castle of Dr. Moledinky.

And the word came back, echoing.

When the last syllable was gone, he went on: "Yes, boys, punctualism; it's what brought us down from the trees, hairy ape-creatures with more brow than brain. It's what gave any living thing a contract to exceed the demands of the outer environment—to punch ahead, if you will. To make the leap, the vast jump, from one state of existence to another. Do you follow?"

I said uncertainly, "I guess so."

"It makes some sense," Pauly admitted. But I could tell it didn't.

Dr. Moledinky ignored us. He was talking not to the walls

of the castle but to the ears of an imaginary audience.

We hung on to the edge of the lantern light, ready at any moment to drop into the dark and flee. I wanted to—and I knew Pauly did, too, because he kept backing away from Dr. Moledinky.

"You may consider this analogy, if you like," he said in his auditorium voice. "The rat on the island lives and breeds and makes a territory all to itself, until one day a stray cat washes up on a piece of driftwood. And then—"

He drew a deep breath, recoiled on his heels, then pitched forward, clutching the imaginary podium, and boomed: "And then, miracle of miracles, the rat, our little pampered, unpestered pest, king of his lonely isle, suddenly is faced with the greatest challenge of existence, which is—"

Once again he ratcheted his hands together and licked his lips in suspense. "Which is, gentlemen, the greatest of all punctualist acts: the decision of whether 'tis nobler to live, or not to live!"

He spun about in a semicircle, swerved back the opposite way, clapped his palms together, and stared at the ceiling, which must have been a mile above our heads.

Then, lowering his head as if to pray, eyes closed, lips sealed, he suddenly raised himself to his full height, and making a fist with his right hand, he brought it down like a piston on his other palm. The air clapped loudly. Pauly and I jumped, and both of us edged out of the conical tent of light and began to back out of the castle, step by silent step.

As we went backward, slowly, feeling our way, Dr.

Moledinky roared at the audience that wasn't there. "And if," he was saying, "'tis nobler to live, to choose life over death and complete extinction, then it is the brave and cunning rat we must turn to in order to solve the riddle of our own existence. For what then? What does that stultified creature do? Having never seen a cat, but knowing at once that cats spell death to rats, what does that rat do? Punctualist that it is, it takes to the trees, it takes to the water; maybe it even learns to fly. And that, my friends, is punctualism! The readiness to solve the emergency of the ages, to leap out of the known into the unknown. And thus, ladies and gentlemen, let me introduce to you the lobe-fin catfish, which wobbles and rolls, and wiggles and woggles; which breathes with its gills, which has climbed out of its watery element to traverse the land, and become—a land dweller!"

I could almost hear the thunderous applause on his final word. Breath sealed, he bent and bowed. Not once, but many, many times.

Then he covered his face with his hands, just like Mrs. Henshaw had once done, and I heard him say: "Oh, my colleagues—you who scorned my experiments. You who said I was a quack. All of you, every member of the Society of Vertebrate Investigation. Ever since Charles Darwin you have held us back, unwilling to accept anything new.

"Well, let me tell you, when the news of my lobe-fin work reaches the presses, you'll shrink back into your learned cavities, your convoluted shells, your nifty little cubicles of lower learning."

Dr. Moledinky glared at his imaginary accusers, his bottom lip pushed out in a truculent pose, his fists clenched, his eyes fixed, full of unmasked hostility.

Pauly and I, still backing out of the castle, stepped quietly under the archway onto the drawbridge and, finally, into the night, which, mysterious and dark though it was, seemed a lot better than being inside that castle with Dr. Moledinky.

Once out of there, we ran like two deer.

Through the wet grass we dashed. A blinking mist of fireflies lay cloudlike over the moat, but we didn't stop to look at them. We fell over ourselves, stumbling over the stinky patch of skunk cabbage. And kept on running, the soft ground giving way under our heels.

We didn't stop until we came to Mrs. Henshaw's backyard, the forest of beech and oak, the brambles of World War I barbed wire, and there we fell to our knees. We didn't know whether to laugh or cry, so we did both; and at the same time.

I mean, the whole thing was impossible. . . .

We laughed until our sides split—a couple of hyenas, howling and kicking in the starlight. Pauly was still choking with laughter when he said, "I guess that takes care of the last rich person I'll ever look up to."

"Serves us right," I said.

"Yeah. Old man Moledinky's just as cracked as Mrs. Henshaw was, if you ask me. Maybe that's what comes of living alone so much. When we left, he was still talking away to the catfish and cobwebs. What a kook!"

I got up from the ground, brushed the dead oak leaves off me.

"I'll never forget the way he turned around and waved his arms all about," I said, chuckling.

And then we walked back to our houses, taking the separate trails that led each to each. Our yards practically touched one another, with Mrs. Cerulli's garden kind of set in between.

That night, after sneaking up the drainpipe and climbing on the roof to my attic bedroom window, I crept into bed; but I couldn't sleep. How could I? Just thinking about Dr. Moledinky and his empty castle gave me the creeps. We'd thought he was fabulously wealthy. Moledinky, the great scientist, the animal collector, the untouchable guy at the top of the lane, who drove a 1947 mint-condition Buick. He was the one perfect thing in Berkeley Bend . . . and now we had to tell everybody the truth.

I thought about that for a while, watching the stars shiver and shine at my window. Pauly's bedroom light had long since gone out. I lay there thinking.

Wondering. What if everybody in Berkeley Bend found out about Moledinky's castle—all unfinished and desolate inside, with no electric lights anywhere and those blue tanks full of catfish embryos and the moat-crawling catfish—what did he call them, lobe-fins?—flopping around in the wet woodsy night, and him giving speeches to the ghosts that gathered inside his brain?

What if everyone knew that Dr. Moledinky, our model citizen, was nuts? His legend was carrying him along, that was all.

Then I recalled how he had finished his speech. The wandering words, full of unbridled rage. So his associates, or whatever, had scoffed at him. So he'd lost, somehow, his professional standing. So what?

Life is full of tragedy—hadn't I seen my dad's inventions turn to poop in an instant, or get stolen away by patent-robbing attorneys? However, I never saw my dad turn mean, or crazy, or angry. He just went on with his life and work, and sooner or later one of his little tinkerings would turn into an invention that might catch on, and then we'd be financially secure for a while.

I had never in my life thought of Dr. Moledinky as being anything at all like my dad, but now that I thought about it, they were alike in one certain way—they were both men of imagination. They lived, as I saw it now, in their dreams. Only the difference was, one of them was obsessed with a superfish and a make-believe audience and in being famous; while the other, my dad, was content in just going along at his own pace, making a living at what he loved to do best, making things with his hands.

Then I remembered something my dad used to say a lot: "We are cast from the same mold." He meant by that—I could see clearly now—that people seem different, separate, until we look at them closely. After that, you marvel at how alike everybody is, how their dreams for contentment or fame are pretty much the same.

A little of this and a little of that—put it all together and you get a complete person. So there's a little of Tom Sola in Pam Snow, and some of Mrs. Henshaw in Dr. Moledinky.

There's a bit of me in Pauly, and some of Pauly in me. And there's plenty of Bobby the Streak in Joey the Jolt.

And isn't that the way of the world?

The way the cookie crumbles, the piano tinkles, and the blue moon comes rolling out of the clouds?

As I look up, now, at the stars, and feel myself growing drowsy, I know that it's true.

We're all just one person. Or many people put into one. Anyway, I'm not going to spill the beans about Dr. Moledinky being crazy or anything like that.

For if I did, I'd just be telling on myself.

So I fall asleep thinking of Dr. Moledinky's castle, with its snow-capped clouds tangled in the turrets, and down below those gleaming emerald lawns the unfinished shanty of Mrs. Henshaw.

And my last thought, before I drift off, is that the castle and the shanty are one and the same, the millionaire and the madwoman are exactly alike, only one isn't rich and the other isn't crazy.